T0129542

An Orphan's Tale

A Novel

❧

VALERIE MILLER

iUniverse

AN ORPHAN'S TALE
A NOVEL

iUniverse books may be ordered through booksellers or by contacting:

iUniverse
1663 Liberty Drive
Bloomington, IN 47403
www.iuniverse.com
1-800-Authors (1-800-288-4677)

ISBN: 978-1-5320-9151-3 (sc)
ISBN: 978-1-5320-9152-0 (e)

Library of Congress Control Number: 2020901109

Print information available on the last page.

iUniverse rev. date: 02/12/2020

PART I

Early Years

Chapter 1

Sometimes it's best to just start at the beginning. In my case, my story began on a crisp, cool autumn morning on October 1, 1935. I obviously don't remember being born. Nobody does. But I've played out the scene in my mind's eye many times over the many years of my long and sometimes difficult life. I imagined how excited my brother, Jimmy, was, and I am sure my mom was relieved to finally have given birth.

"Look here, Jimmy. That's your new baby sister," said Frank, our dad, as he pointed to the little baby wrapped in blankets. Jimmy, in his plain red shirt, with jeans and little sneakers, stood in awe, looking at his new little sister, whom he would help nurture, care for, and love. However, too young to realize his new responsibilities as a big brother at three years old, he simply stood silently, looking around, and thought to himself, *A friend named Maryanne!*

Yes, my birthday must've been a happy day for our little family. But things changed rapidly after that. My dad fell deeper and deeper into the bottle, and he regularly fought with my mom. It was, after all, the height of the Great Depression. Times were tough all over. My mother, the more responsible of the two, would try to talk sense into him. I was little at the time, so I don't have too many memories of the two of them and their arguments, but Jimmy was at the age where he understood there was a dilemma within our family.

On more than one occasion, Jimmy remembered our dad coming home dead drunk. Frank would stagger up the front walk of our little two-story house and proceed to fall flat on his face, with our mom, Catherine, looking on in disgust.

"Oh my ... Frank ... are you okay?"

"What does it f——ing look like?"

"Come on. Let's get you inside and clean you up."

The scene would play out in predictable form each time. He would fall down face-first, hurt himself, and then get mad.

"What the hell took you so long?" he'd shout.

Catherine would help Frank into the house and sit him down at the kitchen table.

"I had to put down the baby and check on Jimmy," Catherine said as she went to the small powder room down the hall from the kitchen to grab some disinfectant cream and a small Band-Aid.

She returned and cleaned up the blood on Frank's face, then put the Band-Aid on, only to have him tear it off in a fit of rage.

"I can't go around looking like this!" he yelled. "It looks terrible."

"It's only until the cut heals."

"No. I'm not wearing it."

Catherine was used to his little rants. Sometimes she'd get worked up herself, while other times she wasn't in any mood to argue with his preposterous tactics.

"I'm going to head up to bed, Frank. Long day. You should come to bed too."

"Here you go again. Always trying to control me. Well, listen to me. I'm going out."

"Where do you plan to go at this hour in the evening?"

"There's always one place that's open, and that's where I'll go."

Frank turned around, stumbled over the chair, and made his way to the front door. He opened it with the amount of force he used to slam it shut.

At a loss for what to do at this point, I imagined how Catherine must have made her way upstairs and headed to the bedroom, only to go back downstairs to eat. She'd complained about stomach pains for a while, but she wrote them off as hunger. Food wasn't plentiful in our home, not during the Great Depression with a father who drank all the money away. When she finished eating, she felt better but still a little off. She disregarded it and continued upstairs to prepare for bed, knowing full well that Dad would be back. He always came back.

By the time morning arrived, the day's sun was peeking through the sides of the closed shades in the master bedroom. Catherine awoke feeling ill. She reached over to feel for Frank and discovered that he wasn't there.

He's probably downstairs somewhere, passed out. Catherine went downstairs to look for Frank, and when she saw he wasn't home yet, her heart sank. She thought back to the most recent argument. He'd come home drunk yet again, and she'd confronted him. "Frank," she'd said, "you're drunk again. You're spending money we don't have."

My mother worked at Hardwick and Magee, a rug mill in Philly, while my father worked in a mill that primarily dealt with dyes. The dyeing mill closed, and my father was out of work while my mother went on furlough. Hardwick and Magee placed its employees in a temporary nonduty, nonpay status due to the economic crisis. People in Philadelphia suffered dramatically, with thousands going hungry. Some people turned to begging, theft, and scavenging. Makeshift homeless camps popped up throughout the city, the most along the Schuylkill River, below the art museum. Fortunately, my parents, Jimmy, and I did not have to take these drastic measures. However, my family did have its struggles along the way.

As Catherine hesitated in the kitchen, her mind spinning with anxiety and confusion at the fact that Frank hadn't come home, she thought back to that most recent argument, playing it over in her mind.

"I'm spending money?" Frank screamed. "What do you suppose you're doin' every day? Huh?"

Catherine had had enough of his combative ways. She turned on her heel to leave the room, afraid she might say something she would soon regret. Just as she reached for the doorway, a plate flew past her head and splintered against the wall. Catherine looked down at the floor; there were shards of glass everywhere. Only then did she turn toward Frank. She watched him stand in place, heaving, his face red, sweat glistening on his forehead, and that vein bulging out of his neck.

"Frank ... what ... why ...?" It was all Catherine could force herself to say. She bent down on her knees to begin picking up the glass pieces scattered over the floor. Frank grunted his way out of the room with a snarl as he passed her.

"I ... you made me throw that. You're lucky I missed. That plate would have hit you in the back ..."

It was always the same old story for Catherine. Every day was a struggle, and Frank didn't make things any easier.

"Frank, you know I needed a new coat; my old one was torn all down the side, and I used it for the entire winter last year," Catherine had said, not quite as angrily as Frank but on the cusp of her breaking point.

"Fine. Go ahead and keep nagging me then. It's all me, all my fault and doing. You always take the easy way out."

"Frank, it's *your* spending that has us in a financial setback. You're unbelievable right now."

As usual, the argument lasted for several minutes. Then Frank left to continue drinking at the local bar he frequented. Catherine walked over to the window to watch him clumsily walk across the front lawn, back over to the walkway, down the steps, and out into the street. Frank, ignoring any sort of oncoming traffic, continued to stagger down the street to the bar. After reliving those memories Catherine sighed and went back upstairs.

Sleep didn't come. As Catherine lay in bed, she wanted nothing more than to shake those memories from her head. She only allowed herself the ability to do so when she sat up, set her feet on the floor, and walked across the room toward the door. She grabbed her light-purple nightgown hanging on the rack and enveloped herself in its warmth.

The minute Catherine opened the bedroom door to go downstairs, she could hear me waking up down the hall. Of course, this is all a big guess, because I was just a baby, but it probably went the way I have imagined it.

Catherine entered the nursery, noting that I was fully awake. She went to the crib and picked me up. Once Catherine had me in her arms, she checked down the hall to make sure Jimmy's door was closed, which meant he was still sleeping. Since it was the weekend, he did not need to be up for school—the preschool that Catherine insisted Jimmy attend, despite Frank's opposition. As Catherine made her way down the hall toward the stairs, she could already see what looked like a foot protruding out toward the bottom of the stairs, the rest of the body out of sight until she walked down some steps. There he was. Passed out again, right on the floor in the middle of the living room. Catherine walked over to the door to see if he had even locked it. Good. At least he had some sense to close and lock the door. Deciding to leave him there, Catherine would talk with him when he awoke, no matter his state.

Catherine sighed, shook her head, and went to the kitchen to make some coffee. Resigned to the confrontation that would soon come, she went about her business—cleaning the house, sweeping the front stoop, and taking a minute or two to read the paper. While she was reading, she heard Frank groan. She went to him, gently shook him, and said, "We have to talk, Frank. Right now."

He groaned again, got up, and stalked into the kitchen without acknowledging her. She followed him into the kitchen and then sat down at the kitchen table with her coffee. Frank poured himself some coffee and sat down across from her.

"Talk about what?" he asked.

By the end of the talk, Frank calmly stated, "This family is my life, and I have to make more of an attempt to show you all that. So from here on out, I fully intend to devote myself as a father and husband."

Interestingly enough, Frank stuck to his word. Day in and day out, to the best of our knowledge, he remained sober. Catherine was elated because this meant he was around to help raise the kids. It wasn't until a year later, in 1936, that he insisted on expanding the family.

"Catherine, I want to have another baby."

"Frank," Catherine started, taken aback by his wishful request, "I think we should wait a little before we have another mouth to feed. Let's take it one day at a time and go from there."

"I don't mean right now. You had Maryanne, but I think another one sooner than later would help me and my particular circumstances. We've got to try. Look, Catherine. I know money is tight. Certain things have happened and are happening that we didn't exactly hope and plan for. But that's life. I feel that another baby is another opportunity to strengthen this family. Besides, another little one is perfect for Jimmy and Maryanne."

Catherine could tell that Frank was trying to better himself, for his own sake and the family. But having a baby to fix a family, or in Frank's case, his alcoholism, didn't make sense to Catherine. Having a baby should be a mutual decision between both husband and wife, the two of them, a way of sharing their love for each other. She wasn't sure if she was ready for another so soon. She preferred to give it some time and see where life took the four of them.

After discussing it with Frank, he consented to give it some time and agreed that having a baby wasn't going to save or fix anything. Catherine was able to communicate this point exceptionally, without any sort of trouble.

Catherine and Frank went upstairs together. For one of the first times in a while... life was headed. They went upstairs together, and for one of the first times in a while, the two of them seemed truly content with the direction in which life was headed.

The days turned into weeks, weeks into months, and months into one year. Then two years. By the time 1937 arrived, my family had welcomed the newest addition to the family. Baby Kate had arrived. Jimmy was four years old, and I was two years old and no longer the baby of the family. Kate had been welcomed with open arms, and we were ready for another playmate. Our father called to share the news with Jimmy and me, saying, "Hey there! Your mom had a girl! You have another little sister!"

Disappointed, Jimmy hung up the phone on our father, not saying one word. Aunt Florence, my mother's sister, had been watching Jimmy and me while our parents were at the hospital. She went to take the phone from Jimmy to talk with Dad, and there was no one on the other end.

"Jimmy," she said, "did you hang up on your father?"

He replied, "I wanted a brother."

As all kids do, he got over it and was excited when Mom, Dad, and Kate came home within the next few days.

Although we were thrilled with Kate, my mother's pregnancy had been much different from her previous two. This time, she experienced the infamous morning sickness and even some other effects of pregnancy. Fatigue, stomach pains, and food cravings were all new, different from when she carried Jimmy and then me. She was no doubt glad all that was over and done. Now it was time to get back to feeling like her normal self again.

When Mom and Kate were released from the hospital, Dad traveled home with the two of them. He made sure they were okay, and once they were, he went to bring Jimmy and me home from Aunt Florence.

The distance from our home to the apartment complex where Uncle Joe and Aunt Florence Lyter lived was a decent walk. No one owned cars, so people either used public systems of transportation or they walked. Walking proved to be most efficient and environmentally friendly, and it gave Dad some time to think.

Things were looking up, and he was starting to become happy with the direction life was headed. Cutting back on drinking proved to be most beneficial. It wasn't perfect by any means. Sometimes he would get that all too familiar urge, that compulsion … *No!* He would not give in, not this time. He had been doing so well. Even Catherine had taken notice of his efforts and offered him compliments that made him feel good, motivating him to keep going.

Frank stopped though, outside the Bridge and Prat Café. All this resistance, avoidance, and abstinence … he deserved a little break. *It won't hurt. One drink. That's it though! No more than one drink. Twenty minutes tops in there.* With the small validating argument in his head, Frank walked up to the door, opened it, and went it.

By the time he stumbled out of the café, dusk was upon the city. The early-afternoon sun was no longer high in the sky and was beginning to set out over the horizon. Frank, belligerent yet oblivious to the world and his main task for the day, after drinking enough whiskey to intoxicate even the most alcohol tolerant, began to walk back home. Then he remembered something. He turned around with absolutely no perception or sense of direction.

"I'll get 'em, bring 'em right here. Right where I can see 'em." Frank turned around again, this time facing his home.

He spun around one last time, facing the correct direction. Frank staggered all the way to Frankford Playground. This was only a few streets away from his home. He still had some ways to go before he would reach his destination, Aunt Florence's apartment.

"I'll lie here. Let me sit and sit. My head hurts," Frank said to himself.

The park, vacant due to the time of day, allowed him to sprawl out across the slide, looking up at the starry night. He shut his eyes for a moment, then opened them to try to regain his focus. However, again, his eyes shut uncontrollably.

"She mustn't know. She can't." Then with no hesitation, he started to drift to sleep.

When Frank awoke, it was morning. The sun was starting to creep up into the sky, the rays shining down on his face through the trees. He had slept the entire night in the park, on the slide. It is a wonder not one person noticed or stopped to say something to him as he slept.

"Whatever. As long as Catherine doesn't find out what happened, that's all that matters," he said to himself. Immediately, he began to fabricate a plausible, realistic story.

He had to be careful though, since it was already the next day and he still hadn't arrived home with the kids. He thought of Catherine, how frantic she must have been right then, probably not even getting any sleep last night.

"I'm in for it."

He came up with nothing, other than he'd gotten sidetracked, obviously, and hadn't pick up the kids on time from Aunt Florence, who would surely give him a hard time. She had been expecting him.

"What and how in God's name am I supposed to get out of this one?"

Frank decided to take action and head in the direction of Aunt Florence's apartment.

He entered and went down the hall to a small window, where the main desk was located.

"Hi, Frank. You here to see Florence?" Jane asked. Frank and

Catherine had become friendly with Jane, the woman who sat behind the main desk of the apartment complex.

"Yeah, here to pick up my kids."

"Okay, I will let Florence know and have her bring them down."

Jane, using the phone on the desk, called up to Florence's apartment. "Florence, Frank is here for the kids if you want to bring them down, or should I send him up to you?"

There was a pause on Jane's end as she listened to Florence. When it was Jane's turn to speak, she simply replied and hung up the phone. She looked at Frank with a disgusted glance, not saying anything until he broke the silence.

"So ... uh, is Florence coming down here or can I go up to her apartment?"

"She said for you to wait here and she would be down in a few minutes with the kids."

"Okay, uh, great, thanks."

Frank waited about five minutes and then saw Florence walking down the hallway, two little ones trailing behind.

"Dad!" exclaimed Jimmy. "Hi, Daddy."

"Did you guys have a good time with Aunt Florence?"

Before they could answer, Aunt Florence grabbed Frank's hand to pull him aside from the kids. Whispering in a most intense voice, Florence said, "Frank, I cannot believe you. You said you were going to pick up these guys yesterday, last night, and you never came. Didn't hear anything from you. I don't know what the hell happened. You're lucky I'm a good aunt to these kids, taking care of them when their own father can't handle something as simple as picking them up."

Frank listened in silence, not saying a word until she was done with her rant.

"Do I even dare ask what happened? Why you didn't come yesterday?"

Still standing in silence, Frank finally swallowed hard and softly said in a whisper, "I had some business to take care of." He did have business to take care of; he had to sober himself up, so as to not let any of this get back to Catherine, the kids, or Aunt Florence.

"And you're a mess too. You're filthy. You clearly didn't even bother to shower or groom yourself before you came here. A disgrace."

"Look. I'm sorry for the inconvenience, Florence. I'll do my best to make sure something like this doesn't happen again."

"You know what, Frank? I've heard it before. Save it. Take the kids and go on your way. I'll see you later."

Aunt Florence walked back around the corner of the hallway, said goodbye to the kids, then continued to walk back up to her apartment.

Frank took the kids by the hand and left the apartment complex, not even saying goodbye to Aunt Florence or Jane at the desk. On his way home with the kids, Frank made it his priority to keep all the past day's events from Catherine. He did not want any sort of grief or added frustration.

It's for the best, for the family, he thought as he continued to walk hand in hand with his kids.

Time passed. The seasons changed, and the summer of 1938 brought us baby Grace, the fourth and final baby of our family. Dad had once again charmed Mom to have another baby. Although he somehow managed to keep the Aunt Florence situation from Mom, he began to slip back into his old ways. Once, he told Mom he was going to the store and would be right back. He did not return until much later in the evening, well past the normal bedtime hour for him and Mom. This tipped off Mom, and the next morning when she found him passed out on the floor, she waited again for him to wake. When he finally did, not in a completely sober state, he spilled details about the day he spent en route to Aunt Florence's, and this, as one can imagine, set off a new world record of a fight between them. I heard them arguing from my room upstairs. I got chills and felt the hair on my arms and neck stand up, and a wave of motion sickness washed over me. I hated hearing and seeing Mom and Dad go at it, back and forth. I did the only thing I could do. I crept out of my room into the hallway and stood holding onto the banister railing. My parents were below and had no way of seeing me. I heard the details much more clearly.

"How could you?" Mom yelled.

"I didn't mean to. It just happened."

"What do you mean *it just happened*? That's ridiculous, Frank. You're ridiculous. I can't believe you did this to us. To our children."

"Oh please. You aren't as perfect as you say you are."

"I never said I was perfect."

The yelling continued for a while, and I had had enough. I went back to my room, softly closed the door behind me, and clasped my hands over my ears. I didn't want to hear any more of it.

It took about a week for Mom to finally say a word to Dad. The two of them eventually made up, and once again, Dad vowed to stay off the booze. He decided that instead of spending the money on alcohol for himself, he would use it on the family. That was when he came up with a new family tradition. On the weekends, he would take everyone to the movies.

On Frankford Avenue, right on the corner, movies played for only a nickel. Within walking distance from our home, we would venture out and walk right up to the theater, Dad fumbling for his wallet until he had a steady enough hand to present the money. We kids would make a dash for the lobby, where they sold snacks. We would put our tiny hands up against the glass, leaving little prints as we gawked with wide eyes.

"Come on, kids. We don't want to miss the show. We have to make sure we get good seats," Mom said.

"All right. Who's ready for some action?" Dad said, placing his wallet back in his jean pocket.

"Me!"

"I am!"

"Yeah!"

Even little Grace gave a smile of satisfaction, unable to voice her excitement.

Once inside, the theater was so packed there were kids sitting in the aisles, while parents or guardians filled up the seats. Looking around the room, Mom spotted an open area of seats. Mom, Jimmy, and I sat in our own, while Kate and Grace sat on Dad's and Mom's laps. They were too young to sit on the floor by themselves. The movie started, and the audience enjoyed the show.

When the movie ended, the audience gave a warm appreciation for the show, clapping as they made their way to the exits.

"What did you guys think?"

"Great!"

"Can we stay longer?"

"I don't want to leave."

The only one who didn't have a comment to make was little Grace, who had fallen asleep in Mom's arms as the movie played.

"It looks like we'll have to get through another week before we can come back," said Mom. We made our way back home.

This lasted for many weeks: work and school during the week, then the treat of going to the movies over the weekend.

When Jimmy was eight, I was six, Kate was four, and Grace was eighteen months old, our family outings came to a halt. What we were about to learn would forever change our lives. From my perspective, life would never be the same again for me or our family.

Chapter 2

When Jimmy and I came home from school, my mom was lying on the small bed in the living room that had been there for weeks, a row of medicine bottles on the coffee table next to her. This seemed to be her new place to sleep, day and night. Between the doctor appointments and her tiredness, it sometimes felt as though she was barely there at all, even though she was right there in front of me. Now our dad had to pick us up from school, which was not always easy because he walked crooked and fell on occasion. Sometimes he sang, and sometimes he shouted and got angry. And he smelled funny.

As had become the usual, Dad stumbled through the door with Jimmy and me after the school day. Kate and baby Grace were, of course, too little to go to school yet.

"Hello. How was your day?" asked an anxious Mom.

"Good! I learned my times tables today," said an excited Jimmy.

"I went to the library and got this book," I said, showing my mother. I paused, then asked the question I'd been wondering about for quite a while. "Mommy, why are you sleeping downstairs now?"

"The doctor says it's for the best, Maryanne." She yawned. "Mommy is tired, and it's hard to get upstairs now. I need a little rest. That's all."

It seemed like ever since that day when she came home from the doctor looking sad, this bed in our living room was where she remained, except when she visited the bathroom. She'd had a stomachache and had been throwing up and sleeping a lot before she saw the doctor. It was strange because the rest of us didn't catch it from her the way we usually did when Jimmy or I came home sick.

Looking at her now, this didn't look like the kind of stomachache Jimmy, Kate, or I got. She seemed thinner and paler since that first time she came home from the doctor. Her clothes were loose, and the color of her skin looked like someone had scribbled chalk on it. Of course, at my young age, I didn't know what stomach cancer was. I didn't know that the disease was killing our mom right before our eyes.

Jimmy came over and rested his hand on Mom's head. "I'll take care of you, Mommy. Maryanne can help."

Mom tried to smile, but her eyes were wet, and she turned her head.

Jimmy was eight and I was five. We attended third and first grade, respectively, at St. Bartholomew Parish. We would walk to school, cutting through St. Dominic's Cemetery along the way. That was always my favorite part of the journey. I was absolutely fascinated by the tombstones and giant mausoleums. I took a hesitant but ultimately bold peek through the windows any chance I got.

Jimmy would turn to look at me with a scowl and say, "Come on, Maryanne. We're going to be late. Why do you always have to look in there anyway? It's the same stuff."

As soon as he would start walking away, I would cry out, "Wait, Jimmy! I'm coming."

When we reached school, Jimmy would run to meet up with the rest of his third-grade friends in the schoolyard. I would do the same, only in my first-grade line. I had gotten to know a handful of classmates rather well, but I was still reserved and shy. I would blush when they would call out my name the minute they saw me approaching.

It was a repetitive routine Jimmy and I fell into before school and even on the way home. The afternoon shortcut through the cemetery gave me the same level of excitement and wonder it did in the mornings. Any opportunity to explore the outside world gave me such a thrill.

Usually after school, Jimmy and I would venture outside, especially on nice-weather days, to catch up with the neighborhood kids for a game of stickball or another game. We would throw our bookbags in the kitchen on the chairs and run outside, while Dad disappeared—back out to the bars.

The weather was perfect—not too hot or cold, exactly the right temperature. Birds would chirp in the trees that lined the streets, and the ice-cream truck music could be heard a few blocks away, with laughter and voices from kids up and down the street. Identical, tiny row homes were on either side of the street, each with a patch of vibrant green grass for a lawn. I heard faint cars honking in the distance, closed my eyes, and breathed in deeply the fresh air. I exhaled, feeling my lungs release the air. A great sense of calm washed over me.

"Come on, Maryanne," said a boy who lived down the street with his two sisters. He was my age, six, while his twin sisters were seven. All three of them would wait outside for me, Jimmy, and sometimes Kate to form a team. From there, we would take on any group of kids our age in a game of stickball on long summer days and evenings. In the winter, we went sledding on blissful snow days.

As of recently though, at least since Mom's sickness, I wanted nothing to do with games or fun. I preferred to stay inside with Mom. Looking out the window at the three of them, while Jimmy ran past me to join the fun, made me sad.

Why did Mom have to be sick? When we would go to the movies on weekends, Dad would hold Mom's hand as we walked into the theater, while Mom held Grace in her baby seat. Jimmy, Kate, and I would run around looking at all the candies, trying to see who could pick out the biggest and best ones. I thought of these much better times while staring out the window, watching Jimmy greet the neighborhood kids warmly. They all turned their attention to the window I was looking out. The boys motioned for me to come out, but I reluctantly shook my head no. I wasn't up for much of anything anymore. As I was daydreaming, looking out the window, a faint cry came from the living room. It started to grow louder and louder until it was bellowing. I quickly snapped out of my illusions, turned around, and dashed for the living room.

"Jimmy, something's wrong! It's Mom! Hurry!" I screamed out the window. I was flustered and out of breath. With that, Jimmy dropped the bat and sprinted for home.

When we both entered the living room, Mom was in a fetal position, on her side, with her vomit lying next to her on the floor. Jimmy ran to the phone and called the operator. He spoke quickly, demanding a doctor or ambulance. Within minutes, an ambulance was outside our home to transport Mom to the hospital. Jimmy phoned Aunt Florence, since Dad was nowhere to be found. She arrived in a timely manner. Once she was there, the ambulance personnel said Mom would be taken to Kensington Hospital Emergency Room for immediate admittance and evaluations. The ambulance sped away, the siren blaring. At that point, Aunt Florence turned toward us and said, "Where is your father? We have to find him."

After a few phone calls, Aunt Florence tracked down Frank, who was at the bar. She told the bartender that she needed to speak with Frank, that he needed to come home immediately. Frank was slurring his words, not comprehending anything she was saying and not cooperating. He put up the usual fight, yelling into the phone that he didn't want to leave and how she was ruining his good time. Aunt Florence could only put up with so much before she slammed the phone back into the holder. Aunt Florence didn't have time for this nonsense with him, so she made a couple of quick rounds in the neighborhood to find someone to look after Kate and Grace. The Parker family down the street was more than happy to watch the younger ones. When Kate and Grace were dropped off, Aunt Florence took Jimmy and me with her to the hospital.

The three of us arrived a little over an hour after the ambulance left our home. Now we were awaiting any news on Mom's condition. I sat silently. I figured it was probably best to keep quiet. I sat there, looking around, watching new patients arrive in the ER, with all different types of problems and injuries.

One boy had a huge gash on his forehead, wrapped up in a towel. He wasn't in the waiting room long. In fact, he was admitted immediately after the woman behind the desk saw him. Another young girl came into the ER with a terrible cough that sounded like a severe case of pneumonia. Then a young man holding his stomach. He was hunched over, like Mom before she was moved onto a gurney. He was probably in his late twenties, early thirties, and he kept a constant hunched-over walk toward the desk to check in. He kept saying that he didn't think it was an average stomachache. He had gotten sick a few times before the pain shifted from the center of his stomach to the right side. The woman behind the desk took all his information and asked a plethora of questions before finally admitting the young man to a room.

Aunt Florence, Jimmy, and I sat watching and listening, for it was much more interesting than staring off into space, wondering what would happen to Mom. We sifted through the old, outdated magazines and newspapers on the tables. Finally, after what felt like hours upon hours of sitting there, one of the doctors came to the waiting room to update us on Mom's condition.

"She seems to be doing better, but we are going to have to keep her overnight as a caution, in order to monitor her."

"Okay, but what about her condition? Has the cancer spread? Is it contained to one area? Is she able to eat anything? Keep it down? She hasn't been eating at home and—"

The doctor interrupted Aunt Florence's never-ending questions. "Yes, she is hooked up to an IV to at least keep her hydrated. We have a nurse with her now, assessing her and stressing to her the importance of eating, even though she probably doesn't want to look at food right now."

"What about the cancer?" Aunt Florence asked again.

"We ran some tests and are awaiting the results to determine the best treatment for the cancer."

Before Aunt Florence could say anything else, the doctor turned her over to his assistant and a nurse and returned to the hospital floor.

Walking down the hallway, I saw things I had never seen before. Chaos ensued. Nurses and doctors were running everywhere, pushing wheelchairs and beds and holding onto patients. It was quite the commotion, and by the time we reached Mom's room, I was glad to be there.

"Hi, Catherine," whispered Aunt Florence. We made our way to her bed, and by that time, Mom woke up and stared at us with a dazed look.

"It's so late, way past your bedtime, you two," Mom said.

"We weren't going to leave you alone in here—were we, kids?" Aunt Florence turned toward us.

"No!" we said in unison.

"Where's Frank? Who's with Kate and Grace? Florence, weren't you supposed to be working today?"

"All is fine, taken care of. You rest, Catherine, and get better. We'll all pray for a speedy recovery and your return home."

The nurse poked her head in around the door that was cracked open and told Aunt Florence that, although she understood her wanting to be with Mom, visiting hours were over and it was time for us to head back home. Aunt Florence, Jimmy, and I said goodbye to Mom and told her that we would be back to visit her tomorrow, as soon as we got done with work and school. I was the last to exit the room. I looked back at Mom as she lay in the bed, wishing, hoping, and praying with all my might that my mother would be out of there soon, all better, cancer-free.

The days wore on. Mom was still in the hospital, the beginning of her third week. It was the same routine for us kids: get up, go to school. Whether or not Dad was around fluctuated. Dad sometimes went out the previous night, and by the time morning came, he either hadn't returned from a night of drinking or was passed out on the floor. We would step over him as we prepared for school. Aunt Florence, when she could, looked after us, taking us up to the hospital whenever Dad was nowhere to be found. Sometimes her husband, Uncle Joe, would look after us with Aunt Florence, whenever he wasn't working. By the fourth week of Mom's hospital stay, the doctor had some news.

I sat anxiously waiting to hear how my mother was doing, hoping she would be better.

"It doesn't look too good from here on out. Her body hasn't been reacting well to the treatments, and I reckon she has a little over a month to live," said Dr. Carmichael. He was another doctor treating Mom in the hospital, constantly visiting her and providing ample information. Aunt Florence and Dad looked at each other. Aunt Florence, however, seemed more worried than Dad.

"A month!"

"Yes. Give or take."

"What is that supposed to mean? I ..."

Dr. Carmichael looked at me as I sat in the chair, my feet dangling over the floor. He leaned in closer to Aunt Florence and lowered his voice to a whisper.

"What I mean, Mrs. Lyter, is that Catherine has at most a month to live. It all depends on her body and how she handles all the treatments, not to mention the cancer, which at this point has spread to other organs."

I tried to listen closely. However, I could not make out what he was saying. Was it bad? Did he not want me to know?

Aunt Florence stared at Dr. Carmichael as he further explained the arrangements that the family should prepare, also letting her know that our family had the full support of the hospital staff during the difficult time.

Aunt Florence didn't want to hear any of it. She began shouting at the doctor, the hospital staff, and anyone who looked at her the wrong way as we left the building.

"What are you looking at?" she screamed at patients in the waiting room, fighting back tears that were already welling up in her eyes. The entire way home, Aunt Florence couldn't help but cry.

The next day, back home, Dad told us as best he could what was going on and what was going to happen. Being so young, Kate, four, and Grace, eighteen months, were anything but aware of the seriousness of the situation. Since Jimmy was eight he understood to a certain extent and I at five knew we weren't going to be seeing Mom anymore.

"Can I go see Mom?" I asked Dad.

"Yoouuu wannaa see whoo?" he slurred.

"Mom. I want to go see Mom."

Dad looked at me, said nothing, then slowly staggered out of the room, mumbling gibberish under his breath.

I decided to take matters into my own hands. I called Aunt Florence, who didn't answer. Jimmy had gone outside to play a game of stickball with neighbors in the alleyway. I had had an uneasy feeling while in school. When Jimmy and I got home, he had rushed to drop off his books and backpack so he could play a game with his friends. He asked me to join, but I declined the offer, because I didn't feel like going outside.

"You never do anything fun anymore," Jimmy said.

"I don't want to," I responded.

"Okay. Suit yourself."

Like that, he had run out to meet his friends as I watched from the bedroom window.

I had nothing better to do than wait for Aunt Florence to call and check in on things. That's when I would tell Aunt Florence that I wanted to see my mother.

As if by some mysterious force, I saw a figure walking down the street toward our house.

That lady looks a lot like Aunt Florence, I thought.

The figure approached Jimmy and the rest of the neighborhood kids and then took Jimmy by the hand, and they both walked toward the house. Once they reached the house, I could fully make out the woman's identity as Aunt Florence. She waited outside while Jimmy ran inside. I could hear his footsteps in the hallway. He opened the door and said, "Grab your things. We're going to see Mom."

The journey from home to the hospital lasted about twenty minutes. The Frankford El pulled up to the station where Aunt Florence, Jimmy, and I exited. From there, we entered the hospital.

Once inside, the hospital had an unusual smell, not like it did yesterday. We waited again in the all too familiar waiting room, like the first time we were together when Mom was admitted on day one. Finally, Dr. Carmichael made his way over to where we were seated on the cushioned chairs against the wall.

"If you would like, Catherine is up for some visitors and would love to see you all," he stated.

We gathered our belongings and followed the doctor down the hallway, into the elevator. The doors closed, and he pressed the number four, and as it lit, the elevator moved up.

The doors opened to another long hallway full of rushing nurses, with patients hooked up to monitors and machines. Dr. Carmichael led us to the end of the hall. Making a left into a room, he whispered to Aunt

Florence, "Take your time," before turning back down the hallway and going on to the next patient.

Mom turned our way. She had had her back to us before we entered the room. She was standing, holding on for support, staring out the window, down onto the street at the outside world below. She was hooked up to an IV that was right next to her, with the fluid dripping from the bag.

Aunt Florence gasped. "Catherine! What are you doing? Get back into your bed."

"Oh, Florence, this is the least of my concerns right now, as it should be yours too ... My, Jimmy and Maryanne, look at you two."

Jimmy made a quick movement to hug his dying mother. Tears streaming down his face, he buried himself in her shirt.

"We'll give you a minute with him, Catherine," Aunt Florence said as she started to well up with tears. "Come on, Maryanne. Let's go wait outside the room, and when Jimmy is done, you can go in and see your mother."

After about twenty minutes or so, Aunt Florence poked her head into the room. Jimmy was making his way to the door. Before exiting, he turned to look at his mother one last time, and she gave a warm, soothing smile as tears poured down his face. Aunt Florence embraced him as she told me to go into the room where Mom awaited.

I entered, and Mom was turned toward the window, lying in her bed. She could see outside and seemed not to want to miss anything going on out there.

Walking over to the bed, I was frazzled by Jimmy's departure and on the verge of tears myself. Mom motioned for me to come over to the bed and sit with her. We talked, Mom first telling me her typical concerns. "Make sure you behave. Listen to Aunt Florence, Uncle Joe, and your father when he's around. Be good."

"I love you, Mom."

"I love you too, Maryanne."

"Why do you have to stay here? Why can't you come home? Be with us?"

Mom was silent as she looked down at me. She looked sad, like everything had been drained from her. It was a look of complete despair.

"The doctors and nurses here help me feel better. They know what to do when I feel sick."

"Who will take care of us? What will Dad do?"

Again, her silence was radiant. Mom was thinking over every question I asked.

"Know that you are loved, and no matter how tough things may get, you have the strength to overcome the odds. Even if it seems everything is stacked against you."

Overcome the odds? What is she talking about? What odds? Does Mom know something I or we do not?

"Mom? Will I ever see you again?"

Silence. I didn't know what that meant. I wondered if Mom was thinking about the answer to that question too. Maybe she didn't know either.

"Maryanne, what does your heart tell you?"

"Yes ... I guess ... I hope."

Mom smiled at me, her eyes beginning to fill with tears.

I nodded and then began to cry too while I nuzzled my face in mom's shirt. Mom wiped at the tears with her hands, reassuring me that it was going to be okay.

There wasn't much to be said on my end. My siblings and I were losing Mom at extremely young ages. Mom did her best to calm me down, subsiding the tears for the time being. We hugged each other for a long time, until Aunt Florence poked her head into the room once more. Mom gave me a nod, and I gave her a soft kiss on the cheek.

Aunt Florence gave me and Jimmy specific instructions to wait outside the room while she spoke to our mother. We closed the door and sat down on the floor while Aunt Florence said goodbye to her oldest sister.

"Catherine, I promise I will look after your kids. Joe and I are in a tight financial situation, but we'll make it work. I'll make sure your children are taken care of."

Things got harder to hear after that, as I sat with my arms around my legs in the hallway. A couple of times, nurses walked by. I looked at them, while Jimmy waved them off. Aunt Florence emerged from the room, her face and eyes swollen and red from crying.

"All right, kids. Let's head out. We have to get you home to finish your homework and get washed up and ready for bed."

We went down the hallway to the elevator. The doors opened up to a busy first floor, the mad rush of an emergency room.

We didn't speak as we walked out into the parking lot, toward the bus pick-up station about a block over. Before we turned the corner and the hospital was out of sight, I looked back, counted up four floors, and saw in one of the windows a figure standing and staring. It was Mom. I gave a small wave and was surprised to see the figure return the wave. I could even make out her movements, blowing a kiss before turning back into the room. I stood for a minute, awestruck, before Aunt Florence asked, "What are you looking at, Maryanne? Come on. We have to catch the bus."

I turned to face them as the bus pulled up to the stop. We all got on. Aunt Florence paid the fare. Sitting on the bus, the hospital became a distant building until it was finally out of sight. I didn't take my eyes off the spot until the building disappeared from view. I turned around to face the front, suddenly having a gut feeling that that was the last time I would ever see Mom again.

Chapter 3

Arrangements for Mom's services were settled upon within the next couple of days. She would be laid to rest in our home. Aunt Florence took care of most of the necessities. She made calls, talked with the funeral director, and made sure Mom's obituary was in the newspaper. She watched after us kids, mostly when Dad came home from work and then decided to venture out for the night. Jimmy and I missed school for the entire week after Mom passed. She was taken to a funeral home and prepared to be laid to rest.

Once properly ready, Mom was transported back to our house, where her viewing took place. Our house was in top condition. Aunt Florence had taken the week off from work to make sure the house was spotless. Aunt Florence had a predetermined idea of how things would look. Mom was to be laid out in the living room, in her casket, while the front door remained open, a single file line proceeding into the living room, through the kitchen and the dining room, and out the back door.

The night before the services, Aunt Florence made sure we were washed and laid out our best clothes. In this case, it was our Sunday Mass clothes. She put us to bed early. The first viewing was to take place the following night, Thursday, while the second was to occur on Friday morning before the burial. Since we didn't have a lot of money, a typical funeral was out of the question. All the money went toward Mom's burial in Cedar Hills Cemetery.

As Aunt Florence finished tidying up the house, I snuck into Jimmy's room down the hall.

"Jimmy, I can't sleep. I miss Mom."

"I miss her too, but you should probably get back to bed before we get in trouble."

"What's going to happen?"

"What do you mean?" Jimmy asked. "We're going to stay here with Kate and Grace. Dad will be around, and Aunt Florence too. You heard what Aunt Florence said. She promised Mom she was going to take care of us. Don't worry. When you get back to school next week, you'll see."

"Oh. Will it be okay?"

"Yes, Mar. We have to be strong for Mom. It's what she would want from us."

"Yes, be strong," I repeated.

"Now go ahead. Go back to bed before Aunt Florence finds you and we get it."

I did as I was told. I turned to leave Jimmy's room and then stopped dead in my tracks. I heard footsteps in the hallway outside and muffled, agitated voices. It sounded like Dad and Aunt Florence.

"Stoppp thisss now," slurred Dad. "I won't have thisss in heeere."

"Frank. Shush. You'll wake the kids. I put them upstairs not too long ago, after calming down Kate for the last half hour," Aunt Florence whispered in her most frustrated voice.

"She did thisss to meee on purpose. Leaving meee all alone with them."

"Frank, what are you talking about? I cannot believe you would have the nerve to say something like that."

I listened intently as Aunt Florence and Dad went at each other. I heard Jimmy, rustling a little; he was no doubt as concerned as I was.

"Frank, these kids need you right now. They need their father now more than ever, and you have the audacity to blame this all on Catherine. You disgust me."

"Oh, shut up, Florence!" Dad was now screaming.

Aunt Florence was doing her best to not raise her voice while trying but failing to keep Dad's volume as quiet as possible.

"I can't take this anymore, Frank. Unless you get your act together ... you're heading down a bad road, Frank. You will one day regret your actions. Mark my words."

Complete silence. I had pressed my ear against the door, listening intently. Nothing. After what seemed like hours, the night pressing on, I saw the light leaking underneath the door go off. Dad had probably decided he would sleep downstairs, and Aunt Florence more than likely headed home for the night. I knew she would be back the following day for Mom's services. I creaked open the door, then slowly tiptoed back to my bedroom, down the hall. I passed Kate and Grace's room and noticed a dim light coming from underneath that door as well. I doubled back, making sure all was quiet downstairs before peeking into my sisters' room. Kate, wide awake, lay on her back in her bed, while Grace slept soundly in the crib next to her.

"Kate?" I whispered. "You all right?"

Kate said nothing. She didn't need to. Right away, I could see the stream of tears that had been running down her face. Kate remained silent until I approached her bed and sat on the edge.

"Where's Mom? I want Mom," Kate said.

I was on the brink of tears, but I remembered those words, "Be strong for Mom. It's what she would have wanted." I quickly fought back the urge to cry.

"Kate, we have to be strong for Mom. It's what she would want from us. Can you do that? Jimmy said so, and Jimmy is always right."

Kate looked up at me wide-eyed but had stopped crying. She repeated the words, as I had to Jimmy. Kate lay back down in her bed and soon enough was off to sleep.

I took that as my moment to get going back to my own bed so I would be well rested the next day. I stood up and tiptoed back toward the door, leaving it a crack open, then finally made my way back to my room. Once inside, I closed the door behind me. I jumped into my bed, pulling up the covers before rolling over to my side. I stared at the picture on my nightstand next to my bed. It was my family, after one of those pleasant weekends spent with Mom, Dad, Jimmy, Kate, and baby Grace. We were outside on the front steps leading into the house. It was summertime. Aunt Florence had taken the picture. She said something about it being candid. I was sitting next to Mom, between her and Jimmy. Grace was in Mom's arms, while Dad sat on the other side, with Kate on his lap. It was a great picture I thought. No worries in the world at the time. Even Dad looked so much better than he did now.

I rolled back over onto my other side. I stared at the wall before I finally started to drift off into a dreamless sleep.

Tomorrow is going to be a long day, I thought.

The morning sun peaked through the windows, shining down on my face. I could hear shuffling outside the door. When it swung open, I sat up and saw Dad in the doorway. He was dressed in an impressive suit—a black, buttoned-up, collared shirt with black dress pants, a black tailored jacket, and shined black shoes. He stood for a moment before saying anything. He motioned toward him, finally breaking the silence by saying, "Get dressed and come downstairs. People will be here soon."

He left my room and moved on to Kate and Grace's, doing the same thing. I was still planted in bed, watching until he finally passed again, making his way downstairs. I glanced at the clock on the wall. It said 11:05 a.m. The wake wouldn't begin until six o'clock that night. Why were people coming to the house already? What were they going to be doing from now until the services began? My head began to spin with so many questions. I figured it was best to do as Dad said and get dressed. I would find out soon enough.

After I finished getting dressed, I headed downstairs. When I reached the landing of the stairs, I was joined by Jimmy, Kate, and Grace. I happened to look over at Jimmy, who was staring at the large setup in the living room, right in front of the large window that overlooked the front lawn. Kate and I turned our attention toward Jimmy's startled look to see a truly upsetting sight. Mom's casket was open. An assortment of flowers, in all different colors, surrounded her. I took note of the purple lilacs, Mom's favorite type of flower. The lilacs were particularly close to Mom, while the rest of the flowers surrounded those. We started toward Dad, who was standing, talking to the funeral director, right next to Mom.

"All right, so we are going to have a procession in through the front door. Here they can pay their respects, then move along through the dining room, kitchen, and out the back door."

"Yes. My only concern is to keep people moving, so as they don't cluster around here, holding people up."

"Uh, Dad?" Jimmy said, interrupting their conversation.

"Yeah? What is it?"

"When's Aunt Florence getting here?"

"She'll be here whenever she gets here, which should be soon," Dad said as he turned toward the clock on the wall. It was eleven thirty. "She told me she would be here by noon."

"Oh. Okay. Thanks."

"Why don't you take your sisters outside for a little bit. Sit on the front steps if you want. I can make something for breakfast for you to take outside and eat."

"Okay."

Jimmy turned to leave the room, still holding Grace. I never let go of Kate's hand as we walked out the front door to sit on the steps. Jimmy kept a surprisingly quiet and calm Grace on his lap, while Kate and I sat down in front of him.

By now, the sun was directly above us, keeping us rather toasty.

We were pretty quiet for a while, preparing for what was to happen in the coming hours. We watched cars drive by and people walking their pets. Life seemed so normal. It was a whole other world. People went on with their day-to-day lives as we sat here, living a nightmare, our world changed forever. I began to think about the last few weeks with Mom, how sick she truly was. Not once did she ever complain or display any sort of resentment toward the situation. She held herself together for the whole family. I looked down the street and spotted Aunt Florence coming toward us. I finally broke the silence when I cried out, "Aunt Florence!"

It was the first time I ever spoke up like that. I was usually a shy, reserved little girl. So when I uttered Aunt Florence's name like that, down the street for her to hear, Jimmy, Kate, and even Grace looked up at me like I had lost my mind.

"Maryanne, shh. Don't yell like that!" Jimmy exclaimed. He looked as if he couldn't believe he would ever have to say something like that to me.

Aunt Florence was close now, waving and walking quickly toward us. She was dressed in all black—a black top, with black pants and dress shoes. Her hair was permed, the curls perfectly in place. Not a loose strand anywhere. Her makeup was done. When she was finally within earshot, she asked, "Is your father in there? Did he go out again? Please, dear Lord, tell me he didn't abandon us for a drink again."

"He's inside," Jimmy said.

"Okay, phew. Thank heavens. I will be right back. You guys, stay. Don't move."

"Aunt Florence?" I said.

"What is it, dear?"

"Can you tie my bow?"

Aunt Florence tied the bow on my dress. Once finished, she moved swiftly up and into the house.

Inside the house, Aunt Florence spoke with Dad and the funeral director. With the door open, I was able to hear what was going on inside the house. They reiterated what was to be expected from those who showed up for Mom's services. Other than the occasional snap at each other, Dad and Aunt Florence put aside their differences. The two of them needed to get through this. Then they would keep their distance from each other. This was for Mom. No matter how much the two of them had against each other, especially after their recent argument, Mom needed to be the center of their focus.

The day wore on, and hours upon hours passed by. The road was not going to be easy.

It was five o'clock. The sun was low now, below the set of row houses that surrounded our house. We headed inside, and I noticed people starting to arrive. I glanced at my mother in the open casket. She was beautiful, looking like she was sound asleep. I couldn't help but wish I could go over and wake her up.

I pictured myself walking over and kneeling down, whispering, "Mom. Wake up. This isn't fair. I want you to hug me."

I envisioned Mom waking up and putting her arms around me, hugging and kissing me, and I would never let go. It was the only thing I thought of as I stood far from the casket, until Jimmy nudged me in the side.

"Maryanne? Did you grab the flowers and note?"

I remembered Jimmy putting the flowers and note that he wrote about Mom on the top of my dresser the other day. He told me to bring them with me to the services, to be laid next to mom's casket so he could read something small that he wrote about her. It wasn't until years later, looking back on that day, I was able to see why Jimmy had me hold the note. Jimmy had another idea up his sleeve for Mom.

"I forgot them, Jimmy," I said. "Be right back."

I quickly went upstairs to my bedroom and retrieved the note and the flowers. I went back downstairs to the now crowded living room.

I handed Jimmy the flowers, with the note still sticking out of the plastic. Then I resumed my place between him and Kate. Jimmy handed off Grace to me. Holding her, I took the flowers, walked over to Mom's casket, placed the flowers within it, then turned to face the small gathering of people. As Jimmy read from the note, I noticed him go inside his jacket pocket and pull out a fork. Puzzled, I continued to watch him.

"Whenever I finished eating my dinner, Mom would tell me to hold onto my fork. 'Make sure you hold onto your fork' is what she would say. I never knew why, until I would see the dessert come out and be placed in front of me. Mom would then say, 'See, Jimmy? The best is yet to come.' I am going to miss you, Mom. I love you so much and hope that you aren't sick up in heaven. Please watch over us, keep your fork, and know the best is yet to come."

With that brief statement, Jimmy walked over to Mom's casket and put the fork inside with her. The crowd was overall quiet, with some sniffling. As soon as we settled, Dad spoke, then Aunt Florence. By the time they were done, there was a line out the door, out onto the walkway, ending on the sidewalk.

People filed in, some by themselves, others in small groups. Then Dad, Aunt Florence, Jimmy and Grace, and Kate and I, in that order stood off to the side.

"I am so sorry for your loss."

"Let me know if there is anything I can do for your family."

"Your family is in my thoughts and prayers." All these condolences were offered with a small hug or handshake.

Toward the end of the service, the funeral director went outside to cease the line. When the last of the line entered the house, the funeral director closed the door. The remaining few paid their final respects. I was exhausted, barely able to keep my eyes open. Aunt Florence came over to us after a quick glance.

"I didn't think you would all be able to stand here this long. Good job. Your mother would be proud. But I think it is time you all head up to bed. We have a long day tomorrow. We will be attending your mom's funeral and burial services, which start early in the morning. Go ahead. Go get changed. I will be up shortly to say good night."

Jimmy picked up Grace, who lay on the sofa, sound asleep already. Kate and I followed him upstairs. At the top of the stairs, we went to our respective bedrooms, put on our pajamas, then jumped into bed. By the time Aunt Florence came upstairs, I was the only one awake. I was exhausted, but once I lay down, my mind started racing. Aunt Florence poked her head into my room to see me lying on my back, staring up at the ceiling.

"Having trouble sleeping?"

I sat up and looked at Aunt Florence in the doorway. Although I knew it to be impossible, I wanted Aunt Florence to make things the way they used to be. A small sob escaped me.

"I know things are tough right now, but you need to be strong for your mom. She is so proud of you. I know it."

The tears flowed more steadily. I tried not to cry, but I couldn't help it. The sadness hurt so much I didn't know if I could take it. "I miss her so much already," I said.

"Your mom loved you. She loved all of you guys and couldn't be more happy with the life she was given and the time she spent with you all. Life comes with ups and downs, but it's all how you look at it. Maryanne, remember, life is 10 percent what you make it and 90 percent how you take it. Your mom wanted to give you guys the best life. Her words were to never give up on anything. Follow your heart. Dare to dream big. Don't let little bumps in the road stop you from achieving all that you could ever want and hope for. If you can take it, you can make it."

For a split second, I thought it was Mom saying those words. I knew it was Aunt Florence there with me, but for whatever reason, I could feel Mom's presence surrounding us. This put me at ease, and I finally let go of Aunt Florence. I drifted off into a deep sleep.

Morning arrived, and I was awoken by Aunt Florence. "Come on, Maryanne. It's time to get up. People are starting to line up outside." She left quickly, onto the next room to wake up Kate and Grace. I rolled over on my side, looked at the clock, and then stood up to get myself ready. When I looked at myself in the mirror, I thought I looked okay. I was greeted by a sleepy Jimmy, then joined by Kate and Grace. Together we traveled down the hallway, one last time before we said our final farewells to Mom.

Downstairs, the room was empty but not for long. The line outside was already down the street. Dad was standing by the door, and as soon as he got the signal from the funeral director, he opened the door, and the line filed in the living room.

All Mom's siblings attended her service. Mom was the oldest of nine children. Her siblings, Francis, Anna, Marie, James, Eleanor (Ella for short), William, and Dorothy, entered the living room together. The seven of them approached the casket, where their sister lay. Standing all around Mom, they were joined by Florence, who took the lead in bowing her head. The rest followed Florence. Closing their eyes, deep in prayer, Mom's siblings stood side by side, hand in hand. When they finished, they opened their eyes, stood still for a moment, then went in a line back out the door. People waited outside, since there wasn't much room inside the house. Mom's family stood outside to greet all those who came to pay their final respects.

Nearing the end of the service, the line was nowhere near finished. The funeral director made the exception to allow for an extra hour. We stood alongside Dad and Aunt Florence. We were hugged, kissed, blessed, and shown deep condolences.

It was now approaching the end. The last few people walked up to

Mom's casket and hugged us, and the funeral director escorted them out of the house. The front door was closed now. It was time to go to the cemetery. Before Mom was moved, we all had our final chance to say goodbye. Dad went first, kneeling before his late wife. He closed his eyes, crossed his hands in prayer, and became still. He stood up when he was finished, which then allowed Aunt Florence to have her time with her sister. Aunt Florence mimicked Dad and then finally stood so we could say goodbye to Mom.

We didn't know what to do. We stood, Jimmy holding hands with Grace and me. Kate held my other hand. I looked from side to side at them. Jimmy had his eyes closed, and so did Kate. Grace, being held, was silent, staring at what was before her. I closed my eyes, and instead of praying, my mind began to wander. The moments I spent with Mom flashed in my mind. The good, the bad, and even the ugly, especially when her sickness started to consume her life. Enveloped within my thoughts, I was brought back to reality when I felt a small, gentle pat on my head. I opened my eyes to see the funeral director standing over me. I thought it must be the signal that it was time to go.

Dad led the line outside the house, the funeral director behind him. They met up outside with Mom's family. I was the last of the kids to leave Mom. Startled, I felt someone from behind pick me up and walk me over to Mom. I turned to see Aunt Florence holding me. When I faced forward again, I was right face-to-face with Mom. "Go ahead. Give your mother a kiss goodbye, Maryanne. I know you were thinking about it," whispered Aunt Florence. As she leaned over the casket, she lowered me enough so I could kiss Mom's forehead. She pulled me back up and then placed me on the ground. Taking my hand, she said, "She loved you and all your siblings. She wanted you all to know that this doesn't change how she felt about you and the rest of your family. A mother's love is eternal."

With that, I walked through the rest of the house, outside the front door where Dad, the funeral director, my aunts and uncles, and the rest of my siblings stood.

"What in the hell were you doing in there?" asked an agitated Dad.

He had been drinking again. Aunt Florence was aware of this and simply chose not to interact or even stand near him. There was an unusually large gap between the two of them. He stood seemingly waiting for a response, but I shrugged my shoulders, then looked away, down at the ground, my face turning red.

"Well?" Dad was now swaying.

"I was talking to Aunt Florence," I said softly.

"What could she possibly have to say to you? And not meee?" Dad swayed even more.

For a moment, no one said anything. Then Aunt Florence decided it was best to change the subject, before Dad started to get out of hand. "I think it's time we head to the cemetery. We should beat the rest of the crowd."

Dad turned to look at her, still swaying back and forth, left and right. He finally stood tall. She stood her ground, facing him, until he grew tired and slowly backed away.

"I don't have time for this. I'm supposed to be the best man here."

We watched as Dad made his way toward the sidewalk.

"Come on, Frank. You are needed for this service."

Dad looked ahead and strutted along, picking up some speed. He was greeted by the driver, whose name tag read Clarence. We all got into the limo, and as it pulled away, the funeral procession followed closely behind. Dad looked out the window. So did I. My mind was in a whirl, and my stomach hurt. Dad at this point was so gone. He wanted his fix. His fix for alcohol. Even at my young age, I could see he was not fully aware of what was happening around him, that his wife was about to be laid to rest.

The limo pulled up to the cemetery, and the driver parked. He exited the vehicle first and then rounded to the back side of the limo, opening the door for his passengers. He extended his hand, offering to help Aunt Florence out, then the rest of us, aunts and uncles, each kid being held by an aunt. Dad was the last to exit the limo. Clarence offered his hand to assist Dad, who swung at it, spitting out, "I'm not helpless here."

Aunt Florence whispered into Clarence's ear, "You will have to excuse him. He hasn't been in the right frame of mind these last few months."

"Completely understandable," Clarence whispered back. Aunt Florence shook his hand as he closed the door, slipping a rolled-up ten-dollar bill in his hand. He respectfully declined her gesture, putting the money back in her hand, saying, "You keep it. I don't want it." Aunt Florence reluctantly took back the money and put it in her small purse. She walked over to join the rest of the family while carrying me.

Off in the distance, there was a line of chairs set up in rows, with one aisle in the center. The chairs were facing forward, toward a small podium with a microphone. Mom's casket lay directly in front of the podium, closed with a bouquet of flowers resting on top. Most of the seats were filled, with the exception of the first two rows on each side, reserved for family and close friends. Aunt Florence walked me over to the empty seats and had me sit in one between Jimmy and Kate. She herself took a seat in the row directly behind us, with the rest of her and Mom's siblings. Dad, who insisted Grace sit on his lap, sat on the end of the row.

As soon as the seats were filled, the pastor, in an entire black robe ensemble, walked down the center aisle until he finally reached the podium. He spoke a few words of encouragement. "Even through the darkest of times, nothing ever lasts forever. This too shall pass," he said, looking at the grieving faces of Mom's family in front of him. "Life is meant to be lived, not to simply go through the motions but to truly enjoy the moments that have been shed upon us. God does not ever allow for us to go through something he does not think we can handle. It may seem otherwise, but it is in times like this where true strength is revealed. Catherine lived a short life, but it was full of love. Love until it hurts. For love is the strongest, most powerful emotion anyone could ever know and feel. Love was Catherine's fiercest ally. It kept her going for so long. And it will continue to, in the eternal kingdom of heaven."

I squirmed a little in my seat. I could hear sniffling next to me. I did not dare move my head to look either way. Dad always said it was rude to look back. As soon as the pastor finished his short homage, the first two rows stood up and formed a line, moving toward the center aisle. I followed Jimmy while holding Kate's hand. Our family line formed around Mom's casket. I looked closely and noticed Mom was propped above a hole. Within moments, the casket began to descend into the earth. Men on each side of it lowered it deeper and deeper into the hole until it would go no more. The pastor stood above the hole and said a few more words under his breath. I could only make out some words here and there. "God ... bless ... love ... forever ... amen."

I watched as the people gathered and dispersed. I received a lot of hugs and kisses on my forehead and watched the same for Jimmy, Kate, and Grace. I overheard Aunt Florence talking to some people I had never met before about a luncheon to follow the service.

The sun was high in the sky at this point in the day. Most of the people who came to Mom's service had already left. But our family was still lingering. I sat in my seat, with Jimmy next to me. Kate was in Aunt Florence's arms. Grace had fallen asleep in Dad's arms, draping over his shoulder. I found ways to keep myself occupied. Jimmy and I had an intense game of thumb war before Aunt Florence finally came over to us with Uncle Joe.

"All right. Who's ready to head out?"

With that, Dad jumped up startling Grace, who was in a deep sleep. She stared wide-eyed at her surroundings before letting out a small cry.

"Aunt Florence, I'm hungry. Can we eat something?" I felt my stomach rumble at the exact moment I asked her.

"Frank, what has gotten into you? Here, let me have her," Aunt Florence said, passing Kate off to Uncle Joe.

Dad stood there before he finally broke the silence with "I'm going to go meet up with some friends. You don't have to wait up for me. I'll be fine. I'll manage a way home." He staggered off into the distance, leaving Aunt Florence, Uncle Joe, and us looking after him. Aunt Florence and Uncle Joe gathered us in the back of the limo.

"Yes, Maryanne. We are going to a luncheon with everyone who attended your mother's services today. We will eat once we get there. Let's go."

Chapter 4

In the months after Mom's passing, we resumed school as Aunt Florence did her best to help us adjust to our normal routine again. Dad continued to display his usual behavior, drinking excessively to the point where he now depended on alcohol. He went out more and more, coming home in the early-morning hours, sometimes not even at all. There were times no one would hear from Dad for a couple of days. Once, Aunt Florence had been minding us kids. She began to worry when she hadn't seen or heard from Dad in three days. By the afternoon of the third day, she had Joe go out to look for him. Within a few hours, Joe returned with Dad stumbling along beside him. Joe took Dad upstairs into his bedroom and made sure Dad lay down on the bed before closing the door behind him. Aunt Florence was downstairs, and as soon as Joe entered the room, she pressed him for answers.

"I found him down the alley, leaning against the wall, passed out. There was trash, empty cans, bottles all around him. It looked like he was homeless," Joe said quietly.

"We have to do something about this, Joe. These kids need a stable environment. Frank isn't providing for them. He's causing more damage than good." Aunt Florence fought back tears as she spoke to Joe.

For a few moments, the two of them sat at the table in silence, pondering what to do, how to handle this situation. Jimmy and I were in the other room and pressed our ears against the wall to hear what Uncle Joe and Aunt Florence were saying. After some time, Uncle Joe spoke up.

"All right, Florence. I'm heading back home. It's getting late."

"What are we supposed to do, Joe? We can't leave the kids here!"

"I don't know, Florence. We can't take on four kids in addition to what we're dealing with here. It might not sound like a big deal. I know we don't have children of our own, but I do not think this will work. It's 1942! Heck, there's a war on our hands. I could get drafted, called in to fulfill my responsibilities as an American. Times are tough for all of us. We need to make the best of the situation and figure out a solution. These kids ... Jimmy, the oldest ... only nine years old ... without a mother ... and Maryanne ... just six years old ... Kate and Grace ... these kids will never know a life with their mother ..."

I heard Joe get up as he pushed the chair away from the table.

"Quick," I said. "We gotta get back up to bed before we get caught."

Jimmy grinned as we both dashed toward the stairs.

My siblings and I came home from school the following day, noticing that Dad was nowhere in sight. We sat down to complete our homework for the night. When we were finishing up, the front door slammed open. In stumbled Dad. He was staggering, unable to keep his balance. In his hand was his favorite silver flask. His other hand held a bottle of beer. He was slurring his words, unable to form a sentence, let alone carry a conversation. We watched in awe as Dad attempted to make his way over to us in the kitchen. When he finally reached us at the table, he managed to get a few comprehendible words out. "Come ... me ... to bar."

Jimmy shook his head. It didn't take long for Dad to realize his son's resistance, so he picked up the nearest book and threw it at him. Jimmy ducked. The book missed him by inches and landed on the floor faceup, some of the pages now crinkled. When he stood up, Dad was there, pulling him by the collar of his shirt. Jimmy was gasping, trying to get Dad to let him go. Jimmy squirmed free and fell on the floor with a thud. I had jumped up at the start of this, taking Kate by the hand, heading for the door. Jimmy dashed for the door as well when he was free from Dad. Dad grabbed Jimmy from behind one last time. Dad looked at him and said again, "You ... all ... come ... with ... me."

"Dad, why do we have to come with you?"

"You heard me ... you are coming with me ... I'm going to be better ... you will see."

"We want to stay here," Jimmy said.

"And I want to keep an eye on you. Aunt Florence says I'm not being a good father, that I'm never around. But that's a lie."

I could see that he was getting angry. I shot Jimmy a pleading look. "Maybe we should just go with him," I said, hoping to avoid making things even worse.

Jimmy nodded while looking down at the floor. Dad released him and went out to the living room. We gathered our coats and anything to keep warm in the brutally cold weather outside. We exited the house shivering while we walked along the snow-covered streets. Dad led the way, stumbling, staggering, and swaying as he walked. Jimmy, who was holding Grace, Kate, and I slowly trudged behind him. Finally, we reached the bar on the corner. It was a miracle that the bar was even open in the freezing cold weather and snow-covered town. The owners, who lived within walking distance, figured to keep the bar open, as people in the area would want to get out of the house. People like Dad, one of their most loyal customers—regulars in particular—would show up no matter what.

Dad was the first to reach the door of the bar. He pounded on it with his fist, and it burst open. It was dark and somewhat dreary inside. The lights were dimmed low, and not many people were there. I looked around and saw one gentleman behind the counter. It must have been the owner. I watched as Dad went straight to the counter and slapped down a fresh ten-dollar bill. Fortunately, for his sake, he was still working, although his time was limited. Dad always seemed to have enough money to cover his booze. Dad worked in a dye mill and later as a marine merchant (supplying troops during the war) by the time we kids came around and he had a family. Dad told the bartender to make use of the entire bill. The bartender looked at Dad with a wry expression. Turning around, he pulled all kinds of liquor off the back wall, then created different concoctions. I watched as I took a seat at one of the booths with Jimmy and Kate. I just wanted to go home.

Jimmy went to the bar and ordered a couple of Cokes. Bringing them back to the table, he said, "We may be here for a while."

I sighed, picked up the bottle of Coke, and took a sip. I said nothing.

Time passed. It seemed like hours, but maybe it was only about a half hour.

"Hey!" Jimmy shouted.

"Shh," I said.

"Dad! Dad!"

Dad, too wrapped up in his drinks and conversation with the bartender, didn't even notice his son's frantic cry across the room.

"Jimmy, stop. Daddy's going to be mad," I said.

"Maryanne, come on. Let's get out of here. I want to go home."

"I do too," I said.

"I don't care if Dad wants us to stay."

"But ..."

"No, Maryanne. We should go."

"Dad will be mad."

"I don't care. Let him be mad,"

"He'll hurt you again,"

"No, he won't. He won't even know what we're doing."

"Is Dad okay?" I asked.

"I don't know yet. It's hard to tell. We have to look for signs."

"What kind of signs?" I asked.

"Like ... when he looks at you or talks or walks funny."

"He was walking funny on the way here," I pointed out.

"He always walks funny." Jimmy sighed, shaking his head. "I guess we should wait a little longer. Then we can ask him for the key and go home."

And that's what we did. We waited for what felt like hours. We sat at the booth, not even getting up to go to the bathroom. Dad continued to sit at the bar, drinking, talking, laughing, never once looking in our direction. He seemed to have forgotten about us. Kate, Grace, and I were drifting off to sleep at the table but were awoken by Jimmy with a tapping and then a sudden thud on the table.

"Wake up," Jimmy whispered.

The three of us stirred a little, then lifted our heads.

"Dad got up to go to the bathroom. And he left his wallet and keys on the bar. Now is our chance. Maryanne, you go grab the key, and I'll take these two outside. We'll meet you outside the door. Go."

I strolled over to the bar and casually picked up the keys, but as soon as I grasped them in my hand, a strong, firm hand grabbed my wrist.

"What ... you doing?" Dad slurred his words.

I had no idea what to do until finally Jimmy came over.

"Dad, we were looking to head back out. We wanted to hang with the neighborhood kids."

"Oh ... well ... why didn't ... say so earlier? Here ... take keys ... meet you back home ... later ..." Dad's words trailed off.

Jimmy and I looked sharply at each other. Was this too good to be true? Was our dad allowing us to carry the keys to the house and at the same time walk on out of the bar? I accepted Dad's offer of the keys. He placed them back in my hands, then closed mine on top of the keys. Dad turned back to face the bar, asking the bartender for some drink I never heard of. Once the bartender presented his drink, he took one huge gulp. Jimmy and I went back over to Grace and Kate and then together left the bar. On my way out, I took one last look at Dad at the bar. He was sitting, his back to us, waving his arms about, toward the bartender, probably pointing to a drink he wanted next. I turned and left the bar, trailing behind my siblings.

Once outside, Jimmy led the way home. Venturing through the snow was difficult, with the amount on the ground, but also quite enjoyable. My sisters and I kept pace for the most part with Jimmy, but whenever he would get too far ahead, we would secretly plot to gather the most snow in our glove-covered hands and aim for his little head with the winter hat. The first time it happened, Jimmy let out a yelp, but after a few more times, he quickly caught on and joined in the fun of a friendly snowball fight with us. Laughter filled the quiet, snow-covered streets as we trekked along toward home.

Making our way on Granite Street, we continued our fun in the snow.

The street was so quiet as the snow started to fall again. Our voices filled the air. We engaged one another, throwing snowballs as we ran closer to home.

We approached the walkway, and Jimmy reached his hand into his pocket. Fumbling around for a few minutes, he finally realized I had the key to the house. "Maryanne, could you give me the key? I'm freezing and forgot you had it when we left the bar."

I obeyed and reached into my small pocket. I spent quite some time flipping both my pockets inside out, then reaching into my small snow boots to see if I had stuck the key in there. When a few more moments passed, my eyes were wide with fear and starting to fill with tears.

"What's the matter? Where is the key?" Jimmy asked.

"I don't have it." I began to sob.

"What do you mean you don't have it? Dad gave it to you." Jimmy's voice was raised a little, fear and concern filling it.

Tears were streaming down my face as I said, "I must have dropped it somewhere in the snow." I turned away from my siblings, hiding behind my hands.

Jimmy started pacing. He was no doubt thinking of ways to get in the house. Breaking any windows was out of the question. If Dad came home to wreckage like that, he would lose it for sure. Especially in his unstable state of mind, who knew what he would be capable of doing. Standing there in silence, with my sobs ceasing, we decided to head up the walkway steps, toward the house. First, we went around back, running up the back deck steps. We figured we might as well try to see if the door was locked. Sometimes this door remained unlocked simply because no one ever used the door. I yanked on the door. The handle didn't budge. Of course, the one and only time it was vital that door remained unlocked, it was bolted. Aunt Florence must have seen the door was unlocked when she was over and locked it before she left. Jimmy, in his frustration, kicked the side railing of the stairs.

"Great. Now what do we do?" Jimmy asked.

"Shh," I whispered.

We plopped onto the steps of the back deck. Only when it started to snow again did we migrate to the front porch, taking cover under the overhang. Jimmy did his best to keep Grace warm.

Aunt Florence jerked awake at the sound of the phone ringing downstairs. She glanced at the alarm clock on the nightstand and groaned. It was late. Very late. She wondered who could be calling at that hour.

"What the heck?" Joe asked, rolling over to face her.

"Don't know who it is, but it can't be good," she said, fighting back her worry.

She hurried downstairs with Joe. When she answered the phone, her heart sank. It was about the kids. They were at a neighbor's house, a lady named Margaret Rogers, and Frank was nowhere to be found. She cursed as she hung up.

"What's the matter?" Joe asked. "Who was it?"

"Frank's neighbor. She's got the kids. Frank's missing, as usual."

"Figures," Joe said, shaking his head.

"I'm heading over there right now," she said and went back upstairs to get dressed.

When she finished dressing, she kissed Joe on the cheek and told him she'd be back soon. She rushed downstairs, grabbed her coat on the rack next to the door, and left the house. The streetlights illuminated the snow-covered way. The neighborhood was still and silent as Aunt Florence trekked through the night, toward our house.

When she finally reached our house, she found us outside, sitting on the front steps. Relieved that everyone seemed to be okay, she leaned down and gave Jimmy a big hug. Then she hugged the rest of us, noting that I had been crying and that Kate and Grace were barely awake, trying with all their might to keep their eyes open. Jimmy looked extremely relieved to see her.

"What happened?" she asked Jimmy.

"Maryanne lost the key," he said, his voice glum.

"What were you doing out in the first place? It's practically the middle of the night! And where's your dad?"

"Dad wanted to go to the bar, and he brought us with him to keep an eye on us," Jimmy said. "When we got there we wanted to go home."

I bit my lower lip and then said, "The key fell out of my pocket in the snowball fight."

Aunt Florence just shook her head. At that moment, she saw a lady coming across the front yard. She was carrying blankets, and Aunt Florence figured that this must be Margaret, the neighbor who called her.

"Phew. Good thing you're here. I was beginning to worry. Stepped inside to grab some blankets, since they were getting anxious in my house. Once I told 'em you were on your way, they insisted on sitting on the steps to wait for you!" Margaret handed over the blankets she brought for the kids, then said, "Keep 'em. It will do you good, and we have enough blankets over our place to keep an Eskimo in Alaska warm in the dead of winter."

"Thank you for your kindness. It is appreciated," Aunt Florence said, feeling relief wash over her. She also felt rage building deep inside her about Frank. The man was beyond help or hope.

"That's what us neighbors are here for. I don't mind it at all. Heard these young ones out here cryin' and carryin' on. Figured I best go see what was happening and bring 'em in!"

"Well, I thank you for your keeping them warm and safe."

"Sure thing. Now you best get inside before you all get it—frostbite, that is."

"Right you are. Thank you again, and take care."

Our neighbor went back home, while Aunt Florence fumbled around in her bag for the house key. She found it and opened the door. "Go on in now," she said, "and get ready for bed."

She took little Grace from Jimmy's arms and walked inside while the rest of us followed her. Aunt Florence closed the door behind her and noticed the stillness of the house. It was completely quiet. Jimmy was already running upstairs, with Kate and Grace right behind him. All they wanted to do was wash up and get right into bed after the long day. I stayed behind. I went over to the couch and sat down, tears still streaming down my face. Aunt Florence walked over to the sofa and sat down beside me.

"I...I...I'm sorry I lost the key," I said.

Aunt Florence leaned over and put her arm around my shoulders, giving me a quick squeeze. "Don't worry about it, Maryanne," she said. "The only one to blame for this is your dad."

Aunt Florence checked her watch. The bar would still be open, but she didn't want to talk to Frank, not right then. She worried that she might punch him right in the nose if she saw him at that point. She'd deal with him later.

Frank pulled his jacket closed as he staggered up the front steps. The house was dark. He tried the front door and was annoyed to find it locked. He didn't have a key.

Now what? he wondered.

He spotted one of the blankets on the front porch, went over to it, and picked it up. On the small tag of the blanket was the name Margaret. Frank looked up toward his neighbor's house. He threw the blanket back down on the porch and proceeded next door.

He banged on the front door. A light came on in the living room. Then the porch light came on.

"Who is it?" a man's voice asked.

"Frank. Your neighbor."

The front door opened. "What the hell are you doing knocking on my door at this time of night?"

"Where are my kids?" Frank asked, suddenly very angry. He wasn't sure why. He just knew he was ready to beat the man in front of him senseless.

"Your kids got locked out of the house."

"No, they didn't," Frank said, kicking the snow in front of him on the stoop. "I gave them my key."

"Maryanne lost it," the man said. "At least that's what we were told. My wife heard them crying on the front porch. She went to find out what was wrong. Say, what were they doing out so late? They're little kids!"

Frank gritted his teeth. "None of your damned business," he said.

"Go home, Frank," the neighbor said. "Go home and sleep it off."

The neighbor closed the door and then turned off the porch light, leaving Frank standing in the near darkness. He stalked back home, giving little thought to where his kids were, and tried the door again. Feeling a wave of dizziness come on, he leaned against the front door. The bile rose in his throat, and he threw up all over the porch.

"Come on," he whined, "open up!"

Silence.

It was freezing, and he was starting to shiver. In desperation, he smashed one of the side windows near the doorframe, reached in, and unlocked the front door. He staggered inside, closed the door, and went to the sofa. He passed out almost immediately, not caring that vomit covered his pants and shoes.

Cradling Grace in her arms, Aunt Florence got angrier and angrier at Frank as she and the kids walked back to her house. No way was she leaving them alone in Frank's house. There was no telling when he'd show up or what condition he'd be in when he did. She thought of how Catherine would feel if she knew how badly Frank was behaving, and she felt a deep pang of sadness. Sadness at the loss of her sister but also sadness for these innocent little kids.

"What's going to happen to us?" I asked, my voice barely above a whisper.

"Nothing," Aunt Florence said, her heart breaking. "Nothing bad is going to happen to any of you. You've got me and Uncle Joe to look out for you."

"I'm scared of Dad," I said. "He almost hurt Jimmy tonight. He got so mad he grabbed him by the shirt and started shaking him."

Aunt Florence stopped. "He did what?"

"He didn't hurt me," Jimmy said. "He was just drunk, as usual."

"Oh, I see," she said and started walking again, now certain that something had to be done about the situation with Frank and the kids. The problem was she wasn't sure what she or Joe could really do. They didn't have much money, and there was definitely not enough to support four children. She decided to give the matter more thought. A short time later, we arrived at her house. She unlocked the door, knowing that Joe was most likely asleep.

"Now, kids be very quiet. Uncle Joe is sleeping," she said. She got us settled in the extra bedroom. Jimmy slept on the living room sofa. In the morning, she'd get up early to go back home to change their clothes for school. Then she'd see about Frank, if she could find him, assuming he hadn't gone home. If he had made it back, he'd be in bad shape. She didn't want the kids around him if he was likely to fly into a rage. She would find a way to work this out; she had to. She quietly tiptoed over to her side of the bed, so as to not wake Joe up. Nothing good ever came from waking him from a blissful sleep. She got into bed, pulled the covers up, and drifted off to sleep.

Later that week, I woke up and noticed something unusual. I peered over the side railing to see Dad sprawled out on the living room floor fast asleep and ... someone on the couch. *Who is that?* She was fast asleep, taking up the entire couch. *Do I wake them up? No, no way, never. Dad would be beyond mad, and after seeing what he did to Jimmy, I have no intention of reliving that firsthand.* I tried my best to quietly go back upstairs, but my foot landed on the top stair, creating a loud creak. The woman woke up, and I darted back to my room down the hallway. Inside my room, I closed the door. I was not only confused but also scared. I didn't like strangers, and this woman was most definitely a stranger. Looking back on that period of my life, I see clearly that that day marked a milestone in our lives, and it wasn't for the better.

Winter gave way to the spring of 1942. I was old enough to know about the terrible war that was being fought in Europe and in the Pacific. I just didn't understand how bad things were going for the Allies at the time. At home, our situation remained pretty much unchanged. Aunt Florence was around as much as possible to keep an eye on us, but she was also busy with her own life. I knew she didn't know about the women Dad was bringing home. It started with that one lady a couple of months back, and now it seemed like he had a different lady stay over each time he went out drinking.

By this time, he was barely working. In fact, I wasn't even sure he had a job. I knew he worked in supplying the troops going to war, and that was why he was never drafted. With Dad not working as much, I thought he might be around the house more. However, he was not. I grew wearier of his actions and felt responsible for looking after my younger siblings, along with Jimmy. Jimmy, however, soon became friends with kids down the street who moved into the neighborhood. He would tend to us, and then later in the day, toward evening, he would hang out with his friends William and Jim, who were brothers. I never met the two boys but saw Jimmy run up the street with the two of them. I would then finish caring for Kate and Grace.

On some days, I was lucky to have Aunt Florence, who would stop by to make sure we were, well, to put it bluntly, alive. Dad's habits overcame his life, to the point where he no longer had any sense of awareness of his surroundings and duties as a father. Time after time, again and again, he would leave us alone for hours, while he was out drinking his life away, meeting women of all ages, then bringing them home to spend the night at the house. Some women were quiet, while others were loud and rude, so rude they would stumble in, slam the front door shut, and speak beyond any decibel appropriate for the human ear. These kinds of women would startle us. Jimmy and I both knew better than to make a sound or leave our room. I would console my sisters, ensuring they remained quiet, so as not to upset Dad. His rage was out of control when he was drinking. Anything could set him off on a violent tirade.

Tonight was no different. The woman made her way into the house, and Dad, having an off night, started yelling at her.

"You ... stupid ... why?"

I woke with a jolt. I lay there for a few moments, listening to the broken words between yells.

"Nothin' ... I didn't ..."

"Shut up."

"I'll kick you out ..."

They were belligerent sounds and words, and none of it made any sense. I feared the two of them would wake Kate and Grace. I lay there, trying with all my might to go back to sleep and ignore the commotion downstairs. It was nights like these, when the windows were open, that I was sure the entire neighborhood could hear. After what seemed like hours, there was silence downstairs. I took that as my time to drift off to sleep.

Bang ... bang ... bang. I jolted awake. The sun was peeking through the window, and the house was quiet. Except for that *bang ... bang ...*

bang. There it was again. I slipped out of bed, cracking the bedroom door open a tad.

"Hello? Hello? Is anyone there?"

I took a step back into my room. Someone was at the door. But what for? It couldn't be Aunt Florence or Uncle Joe; they had a key and would come in. No one else ever bothered to come to our house, especially now that Mom was gone. I turned my back on the door, confusion and fear gripping me. I slid down the closed door and pulled my knees to my chest.

"Could I please come in? I'm here for service. Cleaning service."

Cleaning service? I thought. We had never had a cleaning service, let alone any type of service done in that house for our family. We could never afford it. Well, that was what Dad always said. I finally decided to wander quietly into the hallway. I stood up, turned the door handle ever so gently, then tiptoed down the hall, stopping before the flight of stairs. In an instant of perfect timing, I saw Dad staggering toward the front door, mumbling to himself along the way. When he finally reached the door, it took him a few tries before he was able to pull it open. Curious, I leaned a little closer to better hear and see.

"What do you—" Dad began, but he was cut off.

"Hello, Mr. McGill. I am here as service, to clean your house."

Chapter 5

I didn't quite know what to make of what I was hearing as I stood at the top of the landing. The lady introduced herself as Lily Marks. She repeated what she'd just said about the cleaning service. I got the impression that there was more to Lily than she was letting on.

"Huh? Service ... what do you mean service?" Dad slurred his words in the young woman's face.

"My company and I have come to clean and tend to your house."

"Listen here ... lady ... we don't need your service. We can take care of it."

"I see, sir. Well, how about we do a trial run, free of charge, and if our work meets your satisfaction, then we stay and continue to serve you at a reasonable price."

Dad stood silently for a moment, taking in what she said. Then in an instant, he stepped back to allow her into the house. Dad staggered back to the sofa in the living room, where there was another young woman on the floor, under blankets.

Lily stepped inside the house, and she was immediately struck by the stench. Trash and empty bottles littered the living room, and there was a woman passed out cold on the floor. Dad had passed out again on the sofa and was snoring loudly. Lily shook her head in disgust as she walked over clothes, plates, bowls, cups, pillows, shoes, and toys. The mess didn't stop there. It went into the kitchen. The counters and sink were overflowing with plates, forks, knives, utensils, pots, and pans. The chairs were all askew, and the table was covered with an abundance of mail and papers. The trash can was filled to the top. Lily finished her sweep downstairs and began to head toward the stairs.

I was still at the top of the landing and saw Lily. Out of fear, I hid in my bedroom. Within moments, I could hear her walking up the stairs and the creaking along the way. I listened intently and could make out the footsteps leading toward my bedroom door. The steps stopped right outside. I shut my eyes tight, and as the door opened, I squinted enough so I could see Lily.

"Hello there." Lily's voice was calm and friendly. I saw her standing in the doorway. I gave a small wave to Lily. Lily inched closer to me, talking in a soothing voice the whole time. "My name is Lily. I'm here to help you and your family. I will be coming around for the next couple of weeks."

I looked at her quizzically. *Who is this lady? Why is she here all of a sudden? To make sure we're safe?* I had no idea what to make of Lily. She seemed nice enough. I had no idea such a service existed. So much had been happening since the passing of Mom. A lot changed since those days when our family would have weekend outings to the movies. Those days were a mere memory.

"I know you are probably scared and confused. I am here to make life better for you and your siblings."

I just stared at her. *What is that supposed to mean? I thought we were doing okay. Well ...*

"It's okay, sweetie. You take it easy. I am going to go check on your siblings." Lily got up from the edge of my bed.

When did she sit on my bed? I thought.

I remained still for a few moments, doing my best to absorb the events of the morning. When I heard Lily walking back down the hallway, I stood up and walked slowly toward the door. I saw Jimmy poke his head out of his room. At the top of the landing, the two of us watched Lily clean. She worked around Dad and the woman, covered in what appeared to be a towel. I recalled when Dad, in a fit of rage, took the towels out of the bathroom upstairs and threw them on the floor. Kate and I, who were downstairs at the time, began to walk over to pick them up.

Dad shouted, "Don't touch ... leave."

"What do you think of her?" Jimmy whispered, bringing me back to reality.

I looked at Jimmy and could only bring myself to say, "She's nice."

We watched Lily work. She did wonders with the place—well, at least from what Jimmy and I could see. She even brought the vacuum cleaner out. She knew better, however, than to turn it on, with Dad and the mystery woman still asleep, for a world war might break out in the house. Lily went about her way, moving from room to room, saving the vacuuming for last. When Lily reappeared from the kitchen, I turned to Jimmy and asked, "Do you think she will stay here with us?"

"I hope so."

We finished watching Lily straighten up the remaining parts of the downstairs, and I felt a small tug on my shirt. Kate was standing behind me, on her tiptoes to see downstairs.

"Who is that?" Kate asked.

"Shh," Jimmy whispered.

Lily looked up at the top of the landing and, in a hushed voice herself, said, "It's all right. You guys can come down here. I've been cleaning all morning, and it's about time these two woke up."

We no sooner began our descent down the stairs when Dad and the woman stirred. I watched as Lily stood over the two of them, waiting to give an explanation about what was going on. When Jimmy and I reached the floor and the loud creak signified our arrival in the living room, Dad's eyes shot open. He lay there for a few moments, taking in his surroundings. He no doubt was still feeling the effects of last night's outing. I could smell him as I slowly approached the sofa. Dad finally sat up in a daze and looked anxiously around the room. He saw me a few feet away from him, looking him right in the eyes, while Jimmy remained planted by the last step. Lily, who had moved behind me, was standing over his female friend from the previous evening.

"Hello again, Mr. McGill. You let me in earlier this morning. I'm not sure if you remember. You were quite tired." Lily reached toward Dad. "Mr. McGill, I work with the most skilled and professional people in the state of Pennsylvania. We tend to struggling families who—"

"Struggling? We ain't struggling. We doin' jus' fine," Dad blurted out, interrupting Lily midsentence.

"I mean who might need some extra—"

"Help? We don't need your help!" Dad yelled.

Lily took a step back away from him, now holding my hand. I moved behind Lily, peeking around her backside. I hated when Dad shouted.

"Mr. McGill, if you could let me explain."

"No. Get out."

"But—"

"Leave before I call the cops on your ass."

I watched as Lily stood, eyeing Dad with a cool expression. By this time, the woman lying on the floor was wide awake, staring up at them but not daring to move or sit up.

Lily walked backward, away from Dad. I followed closely behind. Before Lily opened the door to make her departure, she turned toward me and whispered, "I'll be back soon."

I watched as Lily walked out onto the sidewalk. I stared out the living room window for a few moments, wondering what Lily meant and hoping it was true. I made myself scarce for the rest of the day, and we all turned in early, except Dad, who went out again. The lady had left shortly after she woke up.

The following day, when I came home from school, not only did I notice my father was missing, but another woman was in the house. This woman was similar to Lily. I took note that the house was clean, as she spent most of the day there. How she got in the house I wasn't sure. Dad was out as always. Jimmy, Kate, and I had been off at school, and Grace was with Dad's sister in Somers Point.

This woman in our home was dressed in a uniform that consisted of a royal blue dress, white lace collar, and apron that reached her ankles. She had a small white, laced piece that went in her hair, which was pulled back into a tight bun. This woman, I thought, was different looking than

Lily. She wore a businesslike suit. This woman did not have a booklet but instead a feather duster. She turned around from dusting and greeted me with a warm smile, saying, "Hello there, sweetie. How are you today?"

Shy and unsure of this woman's true intentions, I gave a small nod and half smile back at her.

"Oh, my dear, I'm here to help! My good friend stopped by and told me how wonderful you and your siblings were. I wanted to come over and finally meet you lovely children. Lily said it would be good for you guys to have me around the house. I will be here at least for the next week, doing my best to take care of this beautiful house and children."

With what courage I had, I asked, "What is your name and how did you get in here?"

The woman offered another genuine, kind smile before answering. "My name is Elizabeth Waller. Aunt Florence gave me a spare key."

"She knows you're here?"

Elizabeth nodded. "Yes, she knows she can't come around as much as she'd like, and so she asked me and Lily to pitch in. Is that okay with you, sweetie?"

That was the first I'd heard of it, but I figured if Aunt Florence was okay with it, then we would be too.

Like clockwork, I heard footsteps above, then feet running down the stairs. Jimmy came charging down, through the living room, halting abruptly before crashing into me.

"Oh ... hi. Maryanne. You are home."

"Hi, Jimmy. I met Elizabeth."

"Yes, I met her too when I came home from school. She knows Aunt Florence and Lily! She's here to help us. Isn't that great?"

Things might actually start to turn up for us, I thought. *With Dad always out, we at least have Elizabeth to help us. Instead of those crazy women Dad brings home from the bars.* I never liked any of those women. They were mean, smelled bad, and sometimes got sick. And Dad would leave it all to sit there, never cleaning it up.

"Hey there. You okay, sweetie?" Elizabeth asked.

I nodded. The only thing I hoped for was something better. I was so tired of Dad's long ordeal. I just wanted it to end.

Elizabeth returned the following day, and again for the entire week. Once, Elizabeth spent the night when Dad came home late, reeking of alcohol. He could barely keep his eyes open. I was the only one still awake and heard him come in. Elizabeth had fallen asleep on the couch, and when Dad spotted her, he went nuts. He threw the coatrack and small decorations off the end table. Elizabeth woke with a jolt and took cover behind the sofa. I had been upstairs and heard the smashing. I watched from a safe distance at the top of the landing. Dad continued to throw things until there was nothing left. He collapsed to the floor, facedown. Elizabeth poked her head up from behind the sofa, making sure Dad's tirade was over. I watched as Elizabeth rounded the front of the sofa and began picking up large shards of glass sprawled on the floor. She left the room and returned a few minutes later with a dustpan and brush to sweep up the smaller remains.

I watched Elizabeth settle on the sofa. She sat on the edge of the couch and placed her face in her hands. Elizabeth was saying something. I couldn't quite hear. I pressed against the rail a little farther, trying to make out what she was saying. Elizabeth sat back with her eyes shut, continuing to mumble in her hands.

"These kids ... this isn't the environment for them ... he can't take care of them ... not a chance ... get it together, Liz. In a few days, all will be over ... be in better hands ..."

I took a quick step back. What was she talking about? I heard Elizabeth step on the infamous creak. I bolted back to my room in time as Elizabeth reached the top landing.

I lay in bed and, peeking through one eye, saw Elizabeth poke her head in through the crack of the doorway. Elizabeth slowly shut the door behind her. I sat upright, staring at the door. What did Elizabeth mean? Why was she saying all those things? What was going to happen?

I woke to the sun shining in my eyes, through the sides of the window shades. I had no idea what time it was; it could have been afternoon for all I knew. The house was quiet. I had become accustomed to waking to yelling, loud noises, and a variety of other random activities my father would get himself into after a long night. Luckily for us, it was the weekend, and I was able to sleep in. After a long week like this one, Elizabeth had stayed overnight twice, something that wasn't even in her job description. I liked Elizabeth. She was nice and helpful, looking after me and my siblings, making sure we were up for school, had lunch, had food when we got home and a clean house. I thought back to the past week with Elizabeth, knowing today was her last day. She told me one night, tucking me in, that she had other families to look after, and if she stayed forever, who was going to make sure all the other kids out there had a clean house, food, and someone there to be on watch? I looked at Elizabeth with wide, teary eyes. Elizabeth bent down, kissed my cheek, and whispered, "Don't worry, Maryanne. You and your siblings are going to make it. You guys are going to be okay. I wouldn't leave you if I knew otherwise. Trust me." I watched her walk over to the bedroom door, closing it behind her with a soft shut. I had no idea what any of that was supposed to mean. *So much has happened since Mom passed. Will Dad ever get better? What's going to happen to us?*

I pondered those thoughts but was interrupted by a faint noise outside my door. I was frightened. When all was quiet, I tiptoed over to the door. It sounded like a small moan, a little cry. It wasn't pleasant, and I didn't want to know the reason behind the sound. I closed my eyes and pictured myself running around outside one summer with Jimmy and Kate. I imagined Grace in my arms, sitting on the front steps of the house. Dad was walking with his arms outstretched, anticipating Jimmy and I would embrace him. I stopped in my tracks. I looked around, noticing that Jimmy wasn't next to me. I heard him. He was lying on the concrete, holding his leg, which was bleeding. He had tripped on a piece of the concrete that was slightly out of line. I heard it. That small sound. That small moan of a cry, coming from ... Jimmy.

I opened my eyes and turned the doorknob. It opened enough for me to see Jimmy on the floor, looking down into the living room. I crept toward Jimmy, and when I finally got close enough to him, he looked at me with tears streaming down his face. That's when I saw it. I saw Elizabeth and Dad. They weren't the only ones. Two men were dressed in business attire. The third, another woman, was in a blue dress with a matching hat. Elizabeth was standing there, holding Dad while he let out a few sobs. Dad never cried. Only once did I see my father cry. He had been out of control and yelling at Mom.

The three other people were moving into our house now, closing the door behind them and making their way to the sofa but not to sit. They walked Dad over to the sofa and sat him upright. He was crying, but no words were coming from his mouth, which was even stranger. He continued to look at the four of them standing in his living room. Elizabeth mouthed something to one man, who shook his head in reply. He turned and started to make his way to the steps. When that happened, Jimmy and I ran down the hall to our respective bedrooms, closing our doors simultaneously. I could hear his footsteps in the hall. *What does he want? Why is he here, and what's going on downstairs with Dad, Elizabeth, and those other two people?* I thought. When I heard the steps outside my door, I moved back slowly, still facing the door, as the man opened it cautiously.

"Hello?" he whispered.

I said nothing. *Who is he?*

"You must be Maryanne. Elizabeth told me all about you. She said you were a good little girl."

I was in shock.

"Well, Maryanne, I have some news for you. Today is the day that you will be ... moving to a new home."

What? A new home? What's going on here?

With no time to react, the young man took me by my hand and led me into the hallway, to a sobbing Jimmy and Kate, who looked wide-eyed and confused. The man gathered us up and brought us downstairs. When we got downstairs, Dad glared at the man. His face was so red, veins were popping out of his neck and forehead. His hands were at his side, clenched in rage. I could tell from his white knuckles. Before I could register what was happening, Dad rammed the man against the wall. The stench coming from Dad caused my eyes to water. The house shook a little with the force. I heard glass clanking inside our china cabinet on the other side of the room. Elizabeth intervened in the man's defense, her companion, Mark. Dad finally released Mark. Elizabeth gripped Dad's arm and pulled him over to the sofa.

"Frank, we understand your ... um ... frustration, but you need to see from our perspective. This is not healthy for the kids or you. It's time to let go."

Dad, red in the face still from grabbing Mark, jumped up again. Dad beelined for the door, not even saying goodbye to us.

Elizabeth turned to face us. Mark was still holding his neck from Dad's insane moment. He looked at Elizabeth, then at the other man, Rob, and the woman, Abigail.

Elizabeth finally spoke. "All right. I'm sure you have a lot of questions, and I am going to do my best to answer them. I will start off by saying that you know my name already. I am Elizabeth, and I work for Child Protective Services. We received a call about this house. So we figured it best to check things out. I was assigned to your family and house for a week, and by the end of the week, if necessary, a decision would be made. After a week with you and your dad, I knew this wasn't an ideal environment for you to grow up in. Today, you three will be coming with us. We will make sure you are taken care of properly, whether in a foster home or the orphanage, the Catholic Children's Bureau. We understand that your youngest sister, Grace, is living with relatives in New Jersey. She will continue to live there and will not be joining us." Elizabeth spoke both calmly and softly.

Now it was Mark's turn to speak to a completely quiet audience. "It will work out. You'll see."

Still silent, we only moved when Elizabeth, Abigail, and Mark took our hands. Elizabeth took mine, Mark took Jimmy's, and Abigail took Kate's. In silence, everyone walked out the front door. When we were outside, Elizabeth and I fell back. I took one last look behind me at the house. I had come to call home over the last six years, my entire life. Elizabeth saw me looking and slowed her pace, still holding my hand. After a short moment, I turned to face forward again. Elizabeth walked with me toward the Frankford line. Up ahead, Jimmy, Kate, Mark, Ron, and Abigail kept walking, never once stopping to look back.

PART II

Rocky Road

Chapter 6

I stared out the window as the train clicked and clacked along the tracks. I had no idea where we were going. For now though, we sat in silence as the houses, trees, streets, and people passed by in a fast blur. I looked at my brother, Jimmy, who was asleep against the window. Turning around, I scanned for my younger sister, Kate. When I finally spotted her, she was also sitting up against the window. I was scared. What was going to become of us? Where were we going? The train was taking us away from all we'd ever known.

The train was slowing down. I glanced at Elizabeth, who shook her head, indicating this wasn't our stop.

"Two more to go," Elizabeth gently said.

I watched the majority of people on the train exit. When the train continued onward, there were only a handful of people left. Elizabeth noticed my look of concern and leaned over toward me, speaking in a hushed voice.

"I know, Maryanne. You have to trust us. We are looking out for you and your siblings."

"What about Grace? Is she going to be okay?" I asked.

"Grace? Oh, she'll be fine. Not to worry. She is with your father's sister in Somers Point. They will be taking care of her."

I had no idea where Somers Point was, but right now it didn't matter. All that mattered was that she was safe.

Within the next ten minutes or so, the train began to slow. The brakes screeched. It was time to disembark. Elizabeth stood first, and I followed her lead. Elizabeth gave a wave to the rest of our group sitting a few rows behind us. Jimmy was still asleep, and Mark nudged him to wake up. I spun around to look at Kate, who was staring wide-eyed at me. We waited our turn to walk down the aisle. Elizabeth took my hand and led the way off the train. Behind me, I could see my siblings with the other Child Protective personnel. Elizabeth went down the steps first, still holding me. When I reached the last step, I looked around in awe.

It was busy, much busier than I was used to. I looked at one large, towering building down the street, on the opposite end from where Elizabeth was taking me. Off in the distance, there was a large building that had a circular top. That was all I could see before Elizabeth pulled me along, toward Summer Street. We turned onto Summer Street, stopping right in front of another large building. This one, however, did not have a circular roof. It was pointed upward and had quite a few windows. The design was brick, and the front doors looked as if they were made of wood. A sign above the door read Catholic Children's Bureau.

Elizabeth said, "All right. Here we go. Time to go inside." She led the way again, up the few steps leading to the front doors. She pushed them open to reveal a large lobby. There was a large desk in front of us. No one was behind it, but it did contain many shelves and cubbies with files, forms, folders, and paperwork.

"What is this?" I asked.

Elizabeth looked at Mark, Ron, and Abigail, who said nothing. After a few moments, Elizabeth answered my question. "This is the Catholic Children's Bureau. This is where you and your brother and sister are going to stay for a little bit."

The ceiling was tall, and there were large steps off to the side of the main desk, leading to a hallway that wrapped around the foyer we were standing in. Elizabeth motioned for us to make our way to the desk. There was a tiny little bell that made a *ping* when Elizabeth tapped the button.

Around the other side of the foyer, a woman entered. She was dressed in garbs of black and white. It reminded me of a maid, from pictures I saw in school. The woman approached us, getting closer until she stepped back behind the desk. Elizabeth told her who we were. The nun went right to work. She rummaged through the shelves, then the cubicles. She pulled out papers, packets, files, and forms. After a few minutes she said, "These need to be filled out ... unless they were cleared—"

Elizabeth intervened, cutting her off midsentence. "They are under court custody for now. They are required to attend a session on Wednesday, downtown. For now, they are wards of the court."

The woman behind the counter gave Elizabeth a stern look. Then she spoke with an edge in her tone. "These kids ... they surely will need a place to stay for the next two nights. I will need these forms filled out. Otherwise, they will not be permitted."

Elizabeth spoke softly. "Mark, will you kindly escort Maryanne, Jimmy, and Kate upstairs to their respective rooms?"

Mark nodded and rounded us up, placing his hands on our backs and nudging us in the direction of the stairs. I grabbed Kate's hand. Mark walked up the stairs with us, pointing Jimmy into a room down the left hallway, into the third door on the right. Mark told Jimmy to pick out a bed. A few boys, about Jimmy's age, sat on their own beds and looked up when Jimmy entered. Mark said to welcome Jimmy and be sure to help him. Mark closed the door and escorted me and Kate to the opposite end of the hallway. We crossed the stairs that led to the foyer, and I took a quick glance downstairs. Elizabeth was standing at the desk, talking to the woman behind the counter while she filled out papers.

It was the last room on the right side. Mark opened the door, and inside, the room was full of girls around the same age as me and Kate. Most of the girls were sitting on their beds, playing with dolls or looking at picture books, telling stories or jumping up and down. The room was fairly large, providing for roughly eight girls, then the two empty beds at the far end of the room, closest to the window. This made ten total, with the addition of me and Kate. We stood in the doorway, while the rest of the girls in the room suddenly fell quiet and stared at us.

Mark said, "Girls, this is Maryanne and Kate. They will be joining you for the time being. I expect you all to get along, although I don't see that as a problem. There aren't too many issues among the girls here—"

"Mark ... Mark ... *Mark*." Elizabeth was standing at the top landing of the stairs that led to the foyer. Mark backed out of the doorway, bid his farewell to us, then joined Elizabeth.

Elizabeth walked into mine and Kate's new room. She stated, "Tomorrow, you two and your brother are going to a court hearing with us. Don't worry. It's nothing to be scared about. You will have to answer questions."

Kate and I looked at her, puzzled. *Questions?* I thought. "What kind of questions?" I asked.

Elizabeth paused and then said, "Questions about yourself, each other, your parents, what you used to do when you were home, maybe a few others. I'm not sure what else."

All that mattered to me was getting sleep. The moving around, new building, new bed, more girls in one room, Elizabeth talking about a court hearing ... *What is that supposed to be anyway?*

"Why don't you two lie down? You're going to need it. You already look half-asleep."

We both laid down, while Elizabeth untucked the blankets from our beds.

Before Elizabeth turned to leave, I asked in between yawns, "Elizabeth ... what's going to happen after the court hearing?"

"I don't know yet. We will find out tomorrow."

With my eyes half-open, I yawned once more before finally falling asleep. It didn't matter that all the lights in the room were on, or that the sun was shining through the windows, or that the girls had resumed their talking, laughing, and playing. Kate and I were exhausted after a long morning.

With one quick jerk, I awoke. I lay there, staring up at the girl who had disturbed my sleep. What on earth was she doing? Who did she think she was? Not moving an inch, I asked softly, "Why did you do that?"

"I ... I wanted to find out who you were, and your friend too."

"I'm Maryanne, and this is my sister Kate. I don't know anything about this place or why we are here, but I know we are leaving tomorrow for a court hearing. At least that's what Elizabeth told us."

One girl in the back spoke up. "Wait. Did you say you don't know what this place is?"

I nodded, and the girl continued. "This is the Catholic Children's Bureau. This place is for kids who don't have any parents, no family, nothing. Well, that's what I was told. Anyway, kids come here and live together until we get adopted."

When I gave her a quizzical look, the girl went on to explain. "It means another family who isn't your family at first comes to take you and have you live with them. They become your family."

"What do you mean, no family?" I asked.

"It's when you don't have a mom or dad or anyone to take care of you. I don't know who my parents are. I never met them—"

I cut her off. "I know my parents, but my mom, she isn't alive. We had her buried, and my dad, I know him too. We live with him."

"Well, where is your dad? Why aren't you living with him?"

"We *are* living with him." I couldn't control my emotions. I could feel myself starting to get worked up, and the tears rolled down my face.

I buried my face in my arms as I sat on the bed, knees in toward my chest. I let out a small sob.

The girl from the back pushed her way through the group of girls. When she reached me, she sat on the bed next to me. Putting her arm around me, she whispered in a low voice, "I'm sorry I made you cry. I didn't mean to do it. I wanted to help you know what's going on."

In between tears and sobs, I said, "We ... our dad ... me ... Kate ... and Jimmy ... don't ... know ... what's ... going ... on."

The girl continued to console me. Suddenly there were footsteps and yells coming from outside our room.

I watched as the door swung open, revealing a large woman. She was dressed in a black dress, with a hat covering her hair and a small cross chain around her neck. I had never seen this woman before. She wasn't downstairs. This lady looked mean.

"What's going on up here? All I hear are sobs coming from this room. What is the problem?"

This woman's entrance woke Kate with a startle. Kate sat up quickly and took a look at me sitting with my knees drawn to my chest, arms hugging them close to my body. The screaming woman scanned the room. She started to make her way around our beds. By the time she reached me and Kate, she stopped in her tracks.

"Well, I suppose these two are in for an awakening. Did you girls tell them all the chores they will be responsible for?"

No one said anything. The woman blurted out, "No one? Huh. Well, now you will be responsible for not only cleaning your room but the downstairs as well."

One of the girls by the door unintentionally let out a small sigh. The woman whipped her head around, trying to find the culprit. "Who did that? Who did that? Tell me right now."

A girl by the door knew what was coming next, so she fessed up.

The woman walked right over to the girl, grabbed her by the arm, and dragged her toward the door. Before leaving, the woman belted out, "This room better be spotless when I come in here in the morning. And then I will check that you cleaned downstairs. Understand?"

The girls nodded.

"Good. You are coming with me. For the rest of the girls, be ready to leave by nine tomorrow morning. Understand?"

Kate and I nodded.

She turned on her heel, with the young girl in her grasp. She then opened the door and left, slamming it shut behind her.

"Who was that?" I asked.

"That's Sister Ellen. She makes sure we do our chores and obey all the rules."

I already didn't like her. Why did she have to be so mean? The woman downstairs in the foyer didn't say anything about Sister Ellen. She didn't say anything about us doing chores and obeying all the rules. And why did we have to be ready by nine? Didn't Elizabeth say they were coming at eleven?

"You okay?"

"Uh-huh," I said.

"We thought something was wrong."

"No. I was thinking ..."

"Okay. Well, anyway, we better start cleaning this room if we want to be in bed soon. We have to have enough energy to clean downstairs tomorrow. Who wants to start making the beds?"

Sister Ellen threw on the light switch. The light was so bright it forced me to shut my eyes. I rubbed them back open, then got out of bed. I went over to Kate's bed to make sure she was up and for comfort. I did not like Sister Ellen.

I went to hug Kate as the shades were being drawn up.

"You girls better get it together. Breakfast is downstairs, and it is not waiting for any of you."

Sister Ellen walked back across the room and out the door.

I helped Kate out of bed so we could get dressed. The court hearing was today, and after less than twenty-four hours in this place, I was ready to get out. I found the only nice set of clothes I could find and put them on. Then I helped Kate with her outfit.

When we made it to the top of the steps, I stopped abruptly. Down in the foyer, I saw Elizabeth. Elizabeth gave us a small smile. I tugged at Kate's hand a little, and then we walked down the stairs. At the bottom, Elizabeth was walking over to us, about to give us a hug when ...

"Where is the other one? The boy? James, get down here now."

Jimmy emerged from the hall. He was rubbing his eyes, but he was fully dressed in his best attire. We were ready. For what, I didn't know. But whatever the court hearing would mean to us, it was going to happen whether we liked it or not.

We walked out of the building, only to find that the train wasn't running, so we had to take the bus to the courthouse. The ride was long, and when we reached our stop, Elizabeth paid the driver. She took me, and from there we briskly paced ourselves the remaining nine blocks. By the sixth block, Elizabeth ran. At first, I was okay, but after a few moments, I began to feel tired, and my little legs turned to jelly. Elizabeth stopped to allow us a moment to catch our breath, and when she saw me struggling to start back up again, Elizabeth picked me up. She carried me as long as she could, and then with three blocks to go, she put me back down.

She knelt, eye level with me, and said, "Okay, Maryanne, can you make it these last three blocks? I might need you to run a little so we have enough time."

"Okay."

"Good. Let's go."

Together, hand in hand, we ran. I had to make small jumps, which was equivalent to Elizabeth's pace. I could see the big building that Elizabeth pointed out across the intersection. *Almost there,* I kept saying to myself. Running up to the light, it turned green, allowing for us to cross. We made a dash for the courthouse, stopping a few feet from the door.

We stood, caught our breath, and Elizabeth exclaimed, "Fantastic. We made it with five minutes to spare."

We all went into the building, checked in, and headed to the hearing room. Elizabeth grabbed me again. From there, she pushed open the door and led the way down the hall on the left of the front desk. There it was. The third door on the right. I felt a slight nauseating feeling in the pit of my stomach.

The sun was shining brightly through the windows, and nothing but clear blue skies were visible. Around the room, there were chairs set up with a walkway between the two sides. On the far left of the room, there was a big, long table with a group of about five people already sitting there. Toward the front of the room, there was a giant podium above two smaller podiums on either side. At the larger of the three, in the center, there sat a man. He had glasses and was balding slightly. In his hand, he held what I perceived to be a small hammer.

Elizabeth motioned to keep following her to the right side and to sit in the first row, facing the man. I filed in next to Jimmy and Kate. Elizabeth, Mark, Ron, and Abigail filed into the row after us. As soon as we were situated, the bailiff called the court to order.

Ed, a butcher across town from the courthouse, glanced up from the deli counter as Mrs. Webb came into the store. He'd known her for years, and although she and her husband were poor, they were still excellent customers. He'd even given Mrs. Webb free meats once in a while. He knew that Mrs. Webb's daughter, Catherine, had passed away recently, and he took pity on her. No parent should ever have to bury their child.

"Hey, Mrs. Webb. How is your day?"

She looked at Ed with a small twinkle in her eye. "Good, Ed, good. Thanks for asking."

"The usual? Turkey and ham? Sliced thin? Sandwiches for the grandkids?"

"Yes, please. Thank you, Ed."

Ed went to work, grabbing the turkey and ham.

"One pound of each is enough though, Ed. I won't need a lot for this week."

Ed started slicing and, with his back to her, continued their small talk.

"Oh, that's right. I forgot the grandkids aren't around this week. They were moved to that home. I keep forgetting that. Was it a couple of days ago when Child Services came to get—"

"What? They are where?" Mrs. Webb had raised her voice enough to grab Ed's attention. As he turned around to face her, some of the other customers in the store glanced back.

"I ... I thought you knew."

"I knew nothing of the sort. Who told you that?"

"I ... it ... was ... Oh, Mrs. Webb, I am so sorry. Is there anything I can do?"

"Tell me how you found out. Was it Frank? Lousy man like him can't afford to take care of his own children. Who told you and where are they?"

Ed couldn't believe Mrs. Webb didn't even know her grandkids had been taken away.

"Wait. I thought for sure you knew. How did that information pass right on by you?"

Mrs. Webb was starting to get impatient. She glared at Ed. "Ed, if it came from Frank, please tell me. We don't talk to each other. It was always like that. Our family never associated with Frank and his side. We knew he was no good. But we couldn't tell Catherine that. He was the father of their children, and from what we could see and were led to believe, she loved him. Now please at least tell me where they are."

Ed said, "Last I heard, they were taken to the Catholic Children's Bureau. A group of Child Service representatives took them there. I don't know how long they will be there, but for now, it looks ... permanent."

Ed watched Mrs. Webb drop what she was holding in the small crate and make her way to the door. At seventy-seven, she didn't move like she used to, but with a cane to assist her bad leg, she had mastered getting around with it.

Ed called after her, "Mrs. Webb, I am so sorry. Please ... I ..."

Mrs. Webb was already out the door. The little bell jingled above the door as it closed.

Mother, Anna, Marie, Eleanor, Frank,
Florence, Jimmy, me, Dolores

Aunt Florence,
Jimmy, me and Kate

1932
Catherine McGill, Jimmy,
Aunt Florence

Me

Jimmy, Kate and me

Jimmy and me

VALERIE MILLER

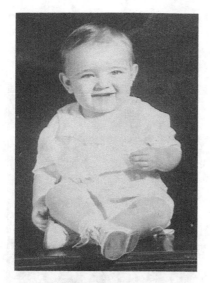

Jimmy McGill

Frank and Catherine McGill

Catherine McGill

Chapter 7

Court had been in session for a little while, and I was about as nervous as I'd ever been. I knew the hearing was important, that it would probably change our lives forever. I knew that even at such a young age. I found myself chewing on my lower lip, a habit I still haven't broken after all these years. I listened to the judge's questions and to the caseworkers who had nothing good to say about Dad. The people in the courtroom gasped when Lily described what the house looked like on her first visit.

The judge banged his gavel. "Order. Order! This court will come to order, or I'll clear the room," the judge said. His voice boomed off the walls and created an echo effect.

"Now, Jimmy, when you were home, how often did you see your father? Did you see him all the time? Some of the time? Or never?" the judge asked.

Jimmy, on the witness stand, sat up straighter, then answered, "I saw him some of the time."

"Okay. When you say that you only saw him some of the time, when was that usually? In the mornings? Afternoons? Nighttime? And when you saw him, what was he usually doing?"

"It was all different times I saw him. When I did see him though, he had some of his girlfriends over. Or he was sleeping downstairs on the sofa. Sometimes on the floor."

"Was he ever awake when you saw him? Not with any of his friends?"

Jimmy nodded. "He was awake, but he would act funny."

"Funny? What do you mean?"

"He would walk funny, or he wouldn't talk much. Sometimes he smelled bad too. He liked to shout a lot too."

The judge asked Jimmy more questions. And then it was my turn. I made my way to the witness stand, climbed up on the big chair, and looked at the judge. I felt queasy in my stomach. I did not like this. I didn't want to be there.

"Maryanne?"

I looked up at him, then nodded my head.

"I have a couple of questions for you, if that is okay."

I nodded. I didn't want to speak, for fear I might cry or—worse—get sick. I allowed him to do all the talking.

"Maryanne, were you ever home alone? By yourself? Or were any of your siblings ever home by themselves? Or was there a time when all four of you were home alone?"

I knew what to say. I didn't want to.

"We were home a lot," I said, my voice barely above a whisper. "But Aunt Florence looked after us."

"I see," the judge said. "Did your dad bring women over to the house, like your brother said?"

I nodded. "Sometimes I'd see them without all their clothes on."

The judge remained silent.

"Sometimes they'd fight with my dad, throw things around. Sometimes they'd throw up on themselves," I said, surprised at how the words just tumbled out. "It was really gross."

"Okay, Maryanne, you may step down," the judge said.

I climbed down from the big chair and sat down next to Elizabeth.

"Ms. Waller, take these children out of here now. There will be no need to question them further, and their presence is not required. Will you and your colleagues escort our young ones out into the main hall?"

She responded with a hasty, "Yes, of course."

Jimmy, Kate, and I stood up from the table. I stared at the people of the court, who had all ceased conversation and were watching intently as to what would happen next.

Elizabeth moved us down the aisle toward the door. Once she reached the double doors, she pulled them open to reveal a busy hallway. As soon as we were through the doors, they closed tightly behind us.

Looking up at the building before her, Mrs. Webb had tears rolling down her face. She couldn't believe it had come to this, Catherine's kids in a shelter. It broke her heart. It was no wonder her family and Frank never spoke. He was a mess. He was scum. Mrs. Webb's other daughter, Florence, had mentioned that she'd tipped off Child Protective Services about the living conditions in Frank's house, but she obviously hadn't been told when, or if, CPS would act. She must have told them she was too poor to take the children in, even with the small state subsidy. Once inside the children's home, Mrs. Webb made her way over to the front desk in the large foyer.

"May I help you?" asked the nun behind the reception desk.

"Yes, I hope so. I was just told that you have three kids staying here. James, Maryanne, and Kate McGill. Is that true?" Mrs. Webb asked.

"Who are you?" the receptionist asked.

"I'm their grandmother. I had no idea they were here. There must be some kind of mistake."

The nun opened a large registry book on the reception desk, put on reading glasses, and ran her finger down the page. "Ah, yes, the McGill children. Yes, they just arrived yesterday."

Mrs. Webb asked if she could see the kids.

"They were picked up earlier this morning."

"What? Where are they?"

"Excuse me, madam. May I please see identification? We were informed that there were no blood relatives to care for the children."

By this point, Mrs. Webb was about ready to throw all the papers opposite her right off the desk.

A woman emerged from behind a door off the side by the stairs.

"What's going on?"

"I am here for my grandkids—James, Maryanne, and Kate McGill."

"Oh, those kids. Yes, yes. They were picked up this morning by Child Services. They had a court appointment."

"A court hearing! I knew nothing about this!" Mrs. Webb said, fighting off the panic.

"As you were just told, we were unaware of any blood relatives other than their aunt, who couldn't take them. And Frank McGill is an unfit father," the woman said.

Mrs. Webb opened her purse, took out her wallet, and showed the nun her identification. The woman studied it carefully. "Well, rest assured any mistakes will get sorted out," the woman said, handing the card back to Mrs. Webb.

"I hope so," Mrs. Webb said.

With that, she headed out the door. She was determined to get to the bottom of what was happening. She also knew deep down that she and her husband lacked the resources to care for four kids, but she pushed that out of her mind for the moment. Better to take one thing at a time.

She boarded a bus and, despite the fact that she couldn't afford it, took a cab for the remaining nine blocks to the courthouse, her mind in a whirl. She had no choice. She couldn't walk well enough to make it with a cane. She wasn't sure what to do. She only knew she had to do something and that she'd figure it out when the time came. She hurried into the courthouse and rushed to the front desk.

"Is there a hearing for the McGill children?" she asked.

The clerk checked her records and said yes. She pointed Mrs. Webb in the right direction. As she walked briskly down the hall, she suddenly stopped dead.

There you are! She walked as fast as she could with her cane. As soon as we saw her, we ran to her, surrounding her amid hugs and tears of joy and sadness. The CPS caseworker stood up. She introduced herself as Elizabeth Waller.

"I'm Mrs. Webb, their grandmother."

The caseworker looked surprised. "If we'd known about you, we would have contacted you. It's funny that Florence didn't mention you."

Mrs. Webb thought it was odd as well. Florence had mentioned calling CPS to check on the kids, but she hadn't mentioned anything about them being taken away from Frank. Thinking it through, it occurred to her that Florence didn't know anything about what was happening, and she therefore had no reason to talk to CPS about alternative living arrangements. At least not until a determination was made that it was necessary for our protection.

"Does Florence know you took the kids?"

"No, we haven't told her about this. No reason to. She did tell us she couldn't afford to take them in, if it became necessary."

"Oh," Mrs. Webb said.

"I wanna go home," I said.

"Me too," Jimmy said.

"We'll see about that," Mrs. Webb said. "That's why I'm here. To come get you. I only just found out this morning by accident that you'd been taken."

Suddenly, Frank burst through the doors of the courthouse, out of breath and looking like he'd slept in his clothes. He came up to the group, glared at Mrs. Webb and the caseworker, and said, "Come on, kids. You're comin' with me."

"Oh no they aren't," Elizabeth said. "The court will decide what happens here, not you."

"The hell it will!" Frank said.

Mrs. Webb leaned on her cane and glared back at him. "Frank, please. Show some respect, why don't you."

"As family members, your voices should be heard," Elizabeth said. "Go inside. The hearing is still in progress."

Mrs. Webb and Frank went inside the hearing room. A short time later, they came out again. Frank stalked out of the building without saying a word to anyone.

"Well," Elizabeth asked, "how did it go?"

Mrs. Webb smiled slightly. "The judge has agreed to an arrangement."

She explained that Jimmy would go with his godparents, Aunt Florence and Uncle Joe. I would go with my godparents, Aunt Agnes and Uncle James. Kate would go to a close family friend's home, the Hellers. The Hellers owned spacious land and a junkyard. It came to be known as Hellers' Junkyard. Mrs. Webb knew it would be a financial strain on Florence to take Jimmy in, but they could manage taking in one kid. Four was out of the question, but one was doable. She wished she could take in one of the kids, but she was too old, frail, and poor to do it.

Everything happened fast after the hearing. We went to stay briefly at Grandma Webb's house before we moved to our respective new homes. While I knew I would miss my siblings, I also knew I'd see them often. I was happy that I wouldn't have to live with my dad anymore. On the day we were to be picked up, we all waited anxiously in Grandma's living room. I tried to occupy myself with some dolls, but my mind kept wandering to thoughts of my future and the futures of my siblings.

Aunt Florence and Uncle Joe were the first to arrive. We all crowded together to give hugs and kisses. There were plenty of tears too. Aunt Florence planted a kiss on each of our cheeks, leaving light lipstick prints on our faces. I began rubbing my cheek to rid it of the mark. Jimmy and Kate didn't seem to care that much.

"All right, Joe ... Jimmy. It's best we head out. We have some things to do around the house."

Jimmy walked over to Aunt Florence and hugged her tightly, and she placed a hand on his head. "Here we go. Let's say goodbye to Grandma and Grandpa and your sisters."

Jimmy hugged and kissed our grandparents goodbye. When he was finished, Jimmy turned toward Kate and me. He was leaving. Reality hadn't set in for me—not yet at least. I looked at this as more of a mini vacation we would be getting from one another. Jimmy walked up to me first and gave me a hug. I wrapped my arms around Jimmy's back. He hugged me tight. Jimmy said something to me in my ear. "Sis, be good. Listen to Aunt Agnes and Uncle James. I will listen to Aunt Florence and Uncle Joe. Okay, see you soon."

He pulled away from me and moved to Kate. Jimmy said something in Kate's ear as well. I couldn't hear any of it. He was saying it so only Kate could hear.

Not too long after Aunt Florence and Uncle Joe left, the Hellers arrived for Kate. Mr. Heller spoke with Grandpa Webb for a few moments, while Grandma Webb sat next to me. Grandma Webb offered Mr. Heller and his daughter something to drink, but he graciously declined, saying that he'd had a late breakfast. They wrapped up their conversation, and Mr. Heller, his daughter, and Kate left within the hour. I made sure to give my sister a hug. I didn't know these people too well, but I had a feeling I would see her again soon. They left, and when the door closed, the house was much more quiet than usual.

Sitting next to Grandma Webb, I waited for Aunt Agnes and Uncle James to come pick me up. I didn't move from the spot on the sofa, even when Grandma Webb got up to use the bathroom and then go into the kitchen to make something to eat for Grandpa Webb. Grandpa Webb sat reading in his chair until he fell asleep. I only knew he was sleeping because of the snores. The afternoon wore on. At three o'clock, I realized that I had been sitting in the same spot for nearly three hours. I had put my head to rest on the arm of the sofa when Grandma Webb came back into the living room.

"That's it. If James and Agnes aren't here in the next—" She stopped short. There was a knock on the front door.

"Mom ... phew ... sorry ... late... busy ... lost track of time." James was out of breath. "So sorry."

Grandma Webb went over to her son and started to hug him.

"Mom, we are so sorry." James steadied himself and took a deep breath. Agnes embraced Grandma Webb and Grandpa Webb. She also offered her sincere apologies. Grandma Webb pulled James aside. Agnes sat next to me, gave me a hug, and patted my back gently.

"Are you ready? Do you have your things?" asked Aunt Agnes.

I nodded. I felt tired, and I was a bit sad.

"Great. As soon as your uncle James comes out of the kitchen, we will be on our way. Did your brother and sister get picked up too?"

I nodded.

"All right, Agnes. Maryanne, are you ready?" James asked as he entered the living room with Grandma Webb.

Agnes jumped to her feet and brushed off her shirt. "Yes. We are ready."

"Perfect. Dad, it was good seeing you. Sorry we couldn't stay long, and for the ... late arrival."

"Don't worry about it. Things happen."

James gave his dad a handshake and pat on the back.

"Mom, we are getting ready to leave."

Grandma Webb came out of the kitchen with some containers of food.

"Mom, we can't take this."

"Oh hush! I know you better than you think, James. Take it. You never liked cooking, and I know Agnes enjoys my food. There are a couple of meals to save you the trouble."

James took the containers and gave his mom a hug. She grabbed his face and kissed both cheeks. Aunt Agnes hugged both Grandpa and Grandma Webb and thanked them.

"Anytime. Please be sure to eat up. And make sure Maryanne eats plenty too."

It was now time to bid farewell to my grandparents. I ran to my grandma and hugged her tightly. Grandma Webb hugged back just as tightly and whispered in my ear, "Be good. I know you will. Don't ever be afraid of anything either, Maryanne. You can do anything you want, even with life's setbacks. Remember that."

I wiped tears that were beginning to form in my eyes. When I let go of Grandma, I hugged Grandpa. He hugged and kissed me softly on the top of the head. "You be good, and we will see you soon. Uncle James and Aunt Agnes will take good care of you."

He gave me a wink and patted my back. We turned to leave through the front door.

Chapter 8

I started back at school. I had missed several days after my mother passed away, when I was taken from home, when I stayed in the shelter for one night, the day of the court hearing, and then another week while I settled in with Aunt Agnes and Uncle James. Now I was back into a routine at the same school as before. Aunt Agnes would gently wake me, prepare breakfast while she got ready, and then send me off to school. I was like any other kid, with homework, projects, and tests.

One Friday afternoon when I came home, Aunt Agnes was waiting to greet me.

"Hi, honey. Welcome home. Are you ready for a fun weekend?"

I put my backpack on the floor, never taking my eyes off Aunt Agnes, who was sitting on the rocking chair in the corner of the living room.

"I am ready," I said rather dully.

"Why the long face? I thought for sure you would be excited for the weekend. Especially since you will be seeing Jimmy and Kate."

My eyes went wide with glee. "You mean I'll see them?" I could barely control my voice, which was shaking with delight.

Aunt Agnes was beaming from ear to ear. She loved seeing me light up like that. "Yes, sweetie. You will be spending the weekend with the two of them. How about that? A whole weekend?"

My smile spread rapidly across my face.

"When am I going to see them?" I asked.

"Tomorrow. The two of them will be spending the night here, and then Sunday, the three of you will be going to spend the night at Aunt Florence and Uncle Joe's house. On Monday, you will be dropped off at the Hellers' house to spend the day."

I could hardly wait.

"Oh, no need to pack. I put together a bag for you while you were at school today. You are set. I also set up your room for your brother and sister."

I went upstairs to my room, and sure enough, she'd made a makeshift bed for Jimmy out of blankets and pillows. Kate would sleep in my bed with me. I stayed in my room for the rest of the afternoon until I heard Uncle James come home from work.

"What is that I smell? It smells fantastic," Uncle James said when he arrived home.

"I am right here, and Maryanne is upstairs. No need to make a grand entrance," Aunt Agnes would say with a smile. I would smile when I heard him.

"Where's Maryanne?" Uncle James called out.

I knew this was my part—to come out of my room. I ran down the hallway toward the stairs, to my uncle, who was standing inside the door. He put his arms out to catch me as I jumped into his outstretched hands. He swung me around, giving me a big hug. When Uncle James placed me back down on the floor, my head was spinning.

After dinner, I did my homework at the dining room table, starting with my math problems. It was almost eight o'clock. I went as fast as I could, not knowing if my answers were right or wrong. When I was done with my homework, I packed my bookbag, then placed it by the door. I changed into my pajamas, and then a knock on the door startled me. It was Aunt Agnes.

"Did you do all your homework?"

I yawned. "Yeah, I did all of it."

"Good job. You almost ready for bed?"

I pulled the covers down on my bed and jumped in.

Aunt Agnes walked over to me, bent down, and kissed me on the forehead.

"I will tell your uncle James to come up and say good night. You are doing so well. I know things are hard, but you keep doing the best you can. Your uncle and I are so proud of you. Good night, sweetie."

I awoke the next day when I heard the birds outside my window. I lay there for a few moments, thinking about the day and the weekend ahead of me. I would be seeing my brother and sister. I could hardly wait. Then I remembered the shelter. The courthouse. Then Grandma and Grandpa Webb's house. My thoughts turned to my father and then shifted to my brother and sisters. I didn't know when I would see Grace again, or if I ever would for that matter. Grace was in New Jersey. At least that was what I thought I'd last heard. I wondered about Jimmy and Kate. I wanted to hear about their lives in their new homes. I would tell them about mine. I shifted in bed. I rolled over on my side. I usually waited to hear if Uncle James or Aunt Agnes might be up before going downstairs. I never liked to be awake downstairs alone. The thought frightened me. The thought of being completely alone scared me.

Then I heard it. A faint cough coming from downstairs. That sounded like Aunt Agnes. I listened once more for confirmation before I finally decided to get out of bed. I set my feet down on the floor to sluggishly walk toward the door. I creaked it open and saw a light in the living room.

I squeezed out of the room. Walking cautiously, I made my way down the hallway to reach the top of the stairs. One by one, I walked down the steps.

"Good morning," Aunt Agnes said as she looked up from her newspaper.

"Hi, Aunt Agnes."

"Why are you up? You usually sleep later than this. You must be excited to see your brother and sister today."

I smiled.

"I thought so," Aunt Agnes said. "Well, are you hungry? Do you want me to make something for breakfast? That should wake up Uncle James. He has ears and a nose for breakfast."

I requested pancakes.

"Coming right up," Aunt Agnes said as she folded the paper shut. She put her reading glasses on the table and walked into the kitchen. I followed her. I liked to watch Aunt Agnes and help prepare the food. Aunt Agnes allowed me to set the table, placing the plates, utensils, napkins, syrup, butter, cups, and napkins on the table, while she stood at the stove, with the pancake batter ready.

"Aunt Agnes? Will Jimmy, Kate, and Grace ever live with me again?"

"Umm ... well, maybe. I'm not sure yet. We will see. Only time will tell."

I was about to inquire more out of Aunt Agnes when Uncle James entered the kitchen.

"Oh, that smells good. Mmmm, I could smell it upstairs," he said. "Morning to my two favorite girls."

In less than half an hour, all the plates had been cleared. Uncle James sat as his food digested, and Aunt Agnes and I began to clean the table. Uncle James said, "That was so good. Agnes, thank you." He blew her a kiss, then stood to go back into the living room.

There was a knock on the door. I knew it was my brother and sister. As Uncle James opened the door, Jimmy and Kate ran inside with Aunt Florence. We hugged, and then when we let one another go, we went into the backyard. We played outside for hours. We didn't even notice that Aunt Florence had left until we were called inside by Aunt Agnes.

The evening progressed, and before we knew it, the time had come.

"Okay, you ready?" Jimmy asked me.

I nodded my head. I was scared out of my mind. I had never done something like this before, and from the time Jimmy told me and Kate the initial plan, I had been constantly replaying the conversation over in my head.

"Maryanne? Are you all right?"

I nodded my head. Jimmy gave me a long look before he proceeded.

"Okay. You know the plan. When Kate gets out of the bath, she will come in here with Aunt Agnes right behind her. Kate will get dressed, and Aunt Agnes will help us get ready for bed. After she turns the lights off and leaves the room, we will lay there for a little while. I'm not sure how long exactly, but we will wait. Don't move. I don't want either of you to blow it. Okay?"

"Got it" was all I could force myself to say. I didn't like this idea.

"Good. Kate? You all good? You understand what you need to do?"

Kate softly said, "Yes."

"Okay. Now I will keep a lookout. And remember, when Aunt Agnes and Uncle James go to bed, that is when we move out. Aunt Agnes keeps the key under the mat by the door. We can lock up the door when we go out. From there, I will lead us to Mom's grave."

In the darkness, I couldn't see perfectly, but I could make out shadows and hear movements. Jimmy was getting into position by the door. After what felt like hours, I could hear Aunt Agnes coming up the stairs, the floor creaking as she walked. Uncle James was still downstairs. I knew this without even asking. He usually went to bed well after Aunt Agnes. Uncle James was a night owl, especially on the weekends. Waiting for Uncle James was getting harder as the minutes passed. I could feel my eyes getting heavy. However, I mustered all the strength in me to stay awake. The light that was streaming in through the bottom of the door was finally extinguished. Uncle James came trudging up the steps. Now to wait a few more minutes, and Uncle James would be out like a light. We sat in silence and let more time pass before we made a break for it.

At the appointed time, Jimmy said, "We have to go. Both Aunt Agnes and Uncle James are in bed. Let's go."

"Okay. I'm ready to see Mom."

Jimmy led the way through the downstairs, out into the backyard, and across the street. I was the only one with him. Kate had decided to stay home and sleep. Too much adventure for her, I guess. I did my best to keep up with him. He was moving so fast I basically had to run. We moved along the sidewalk into the darkness. Along the way, I noticed the neighborhood seemed not only darker but scary as well. No lights in any of the houses. No one outside. The streets deserted. The only light came from the streetlights. There weren't even any cars driving around.

"We have to keep moving. We are almost there." We reached the bus stop, barely catching one before it pulled away.

When we hopped off the bus, I could hardly breathe. The air was warm, but it took a lot for a six-year-old with small lungs to keep the right breathing pace.

"Here. Through these trees and over some of these tombstones. Mom's should be coming up soon."

Pointing across the way, Jimmy exclaimed, "Right there!"

"What does it say on Mom's stone?"

Jimmy read it aloud:

Catherine McGill, Beloved Daughter, Sister, Wife, and Mother
Life Can Only Be Understood Backward but Must Be Lived Forward
May 21, 1902–September 14, 1941

"What does that mean?" I whispered.

"I think it means to keep moving forward no matter what happens. I remember Mom would say that a lot to herself."

"She did?" I questioned.

"Usually whenever she was home with us and Dad was out. I heard her sometimes. I never said anything. I pretended I wasn't listening."

For a while, we stared at Mom's grave.

The wind started to pick up. There was some rustling of the leaves that were scattered around the bottoms of trees. The tree branches began to sway in the wind, and as I looked up from my mother's grave, I saw it. Something or someone was standing off in the distance. I saw the silhouette. It was tall, and only when it moved did I realize it was a person.

I tugged on Jimmy's shirt sleeve. "Jimmy? Who is that?"

Jimmy looked in the direction that I pointed. He squinted his eyes, then said, "I don't see any—" Jimmy's eyes widened, and he had a look of terror on his face. I immediately felt my stomach flip. Tears were forming in my eyes.

Jimmy and I watched the figure start to move in our direction. We had remained surprisingly still until we detected movement from the figure. Then we ran. We bolted toward the gates that had been left open. I could feel my heart beating furiously in my chest. Jimmy was right in front of me, only a few steps ahead. We were nearly there when I felt my foot get caught in the root of one of the oversized trees. I tripped and landed with a thud. When I looked down to try and remove my foot from the root, I realized my shoelace had gotten tangled around it. I looked up nervously in the direction of the figure, who had seen us run and was staggering toward us. I screamed for Jimmy. "Help! My shoe!"

Jimmy stopped momentarily. "Take your shoe off! Come on!"

I grabbed my foot and pulled the shoe off. I quickly freed the shoe from the root, put the shoe back on, and headed for the gates. When I reached the outside of the gates, the streetlights illuminated the spot where Jimmy was waiting for me. I reached Jimmy, and he took off again. Before taking off with Jimmy, I glanced back. We were safe. The figure staggered and swayed back and forth before falling facedown to the ground. I didn't watch anymore. I ran to catch up with Jimmy and get home. Finally, there were the headlights of the bus. Jimmy ran to the door as it opened and stood waiting for me to catch up. As soon as I jumped on, the driver closed the door and started down the street.

When the driver stopped at our spot, he said, "Last stop."

We ran for what felt like an eternity and reached the house. Jimmy fumbled around for the key. When he got it out of his pocket, he quickly unlocked the door and threw himself inside the kitchen, with me behind him. He closed the door, locking it and latching it with the bolt. I leaned up against the wall, and Jimmy was hunched over to catch his breath.

"Never again," he said.

I couldn't agree more.

"I don't want to do that again," I said, regaining my breath. "Kate was the only smart one. I should have stayed back with her."

"Maryanne, don't say anything to anyone about last night. Not Aunt Agnes. Not Uncle James. No one. That man didn't get us. He was nowhere near us. Okay? Please don't talk ever about last night."

"I won't say anything. Did you see who it was? When I tripped, I only saw him for a second. I still couldn't see who it was."

"No. I didn't see who it was, but I think it was a man."

"I think it was a man too. If it was, did you see the way he was walking? He kept swaying and moving from side to side. Maybe he knows Dad."

"I'm not sure, Maryanne."

"Or maybe he *was* Dad."

"Hey, kids, let's go. You have to be ready to go soon," Aunt Agnes called out.

"We're coming!" Jimmy responded. "Time for some breakfast, Maryanne. What do you say?"

I agreed, and we went downstairs. As I ate breakfast, my thoughts wandered to events planned for the day ahead of us. When we finished, Uncle James accompanied us to the Heller residence. The Hellers lived relatively close to Aunt Agnes and Uncle James, so travel time wasn't long. When we reached their house, Kate went running inside. It looked like someone had made an attempt at fabricating a sidewalk, but the house was built at a junkyard site. Not too much leeway for a cement sidewalk. Mr. Heller continued walking directly for the house, while Jimmy and I stopped at the start of Mr. Heller's best attempt of a walkway toward the house. I looked around. The house was in decent condition. There wasn't much else around, except for the huge junkyard that was across the way from the Hellers' house. There were all sorts of parts, scraps, metals, and trash. I walked around the grounds of the house. I saw some toys along the side of the house that led to the backyard. There was a small swing set and a play area off to the right side. The rest of the yard was used for Mr. Heller's equipment. There was a toolbox next to a couple of two-by-fours that were positioned up by small stands. I noted the saw that lay next to the work spot. After exploring the grounds, I walked into the house through the back door. I was greeted by Mrs. Heller, who was sitting at the kitchen table drinking coffee and reading the newspaper. She looked up from her paper when I entered.

"Hello there. You must be Maryanne. Mr. Heller and I have heard so much about you and your brother, Jimmy. Kate loves to talk about you. Did you have a look around?"

"Hi. I looked around outside. I think it's great."

Mrs. Heller nodded with a small smile. She lifted her paper and took a sip of coffee, then said, "I think your siblings are either in the living room or upstairs."

When I turned around, I got a good look at the living room. The ceiling and walls were high. There were plenty of sofas, armchairs, and couches around the room. There were small end tables positioned next to the furniture and even a long coffee table in the center of the room. There was a black telephone on one of the end tables that was closest to the large sofa. There was even a small square box in the room. All the pieces of furniture were facing it. I had never seen anything like it before. It had two wires sticking out of it, and the front of the box was different from the three other sides. One side was indented and resembled a window.

"You seemed to have stumbled across our TV. Instead of listening to the news on the radio, you can actually watch it."

I had never heard of anything like it before. It sure sounded fun and different, and I couldn't wait to watch it later.

I took one last look around the room, particularly at the box that Mr. Heller kept calling a TV, then worked my way upstairs. I met up with Jimmy and Kate in Kate's room. They were both talking and laughing about one of Kate's toys.

"Look, Maryanne. Watch what it does." Jimmy turned toward me, laughing.

I looked at the toy. It was in the shape of a circle. I watched as Jimmy picked it up and threw it at the ground. In an instant, it bounced off the floor, back at Jimmy. He caught it and laughed again.

"What is it?" I asked as I watched Jimmy shape and transform the circle into another odd shape.

"It's called Silly Putty!" Kate exclaimed.

I loved watching my siblings have fun.

The rest of the day was filled with more laughter. We went in the backyard to play games of tag, hide-and-seek, cops and robbers, and even a small game of stickball with some kids from down the street. The Hellers didn't have a neighbor within usual distance, as they were way up the road on Grant Avenue.

We had dinner together and finished the night with a board game and TV. I had never seen people talking and walking around in a small box. I hoped one day I would have the ability to get one. However, the shenanigans from the previous night left us exhausted. As I started to drift off to sleep, I thought about the next day. I became sad at the thought of leaving my brother and sister again, uncertain if I might not see them for a long time, or ever again. When my eyes became so heavy that I could no longer keep them open, my worries were put to ease, at least until the morning. The house settled, and by midnight, there was complete silence in the Hellers' residence.

Chapter 9

For the next couple of months, all I did was get up, go to school, come home, do homework and chores, eat dinner, then go to bed. The winter months in Philadelphia were upon us, which left a bitter cold in the air. I didn't see much of my dad. He was out in the streets by this time. Dad rarely ever showed up to see us, not even for the holidays. The days were short, the nights were long, and I only had the fast-approaching holidays to look forward to. Thanksgiving at Aunt Agnes and Uncle James's was nice. They had invited Aunt Agnes's family over for dinner.

In the short month ahead, lights, shopping, decorating, baking, and gifts took over not only our house but school, stores, and the neighborhood. Christmas was almost here. I kept my list short. Like Thanksgiving, Christmas came and went in the blink of an eye. For Christmas dinner, I got to see Jimmy. We showed off our new toys and clothes. We were impressed and picked up right where we left off, laughing. On the way home, I noticed something was different. Aunt Agnes and Uncle James weren't talking to each other. They were usually chatty with each other. They took turns tucking me in for the night, kissing my forehead, and wishing me a merry Christmas. I didn't know what it was, but something was wrong.

Nothing seemed out of the ordinary during that week following

Christmas, which eased my mind. That is until Aunt Agnes came to me on New Year's Eve.

"Maryanne, dear, are you ready for the party? We will be leaving within the hour. You should look your best. It's New Year's, after all."

"Yes, Aunt Agnes. I'll change."

"I think you should try wearing one of those nice shirts you got for Christmas. One of them would look nice."

I went to the Christmas tree and began looking for the right shirt. A long-sleeve, light shirt, a solid red color. It had a small snowman on the front of it. The snowman had tiny black eyes, a carrot for a nose, a smile made out of small black stones, and a scarf. It was holding a broomstick. I liked the shirt, so I decided that would be the one I would wear to the party.

A little before four o'clock, Aunt Agnes said that we should go to Mass, like we did on Christmas. It was a holy day, she said.

The three of us were off for the 4:30 p.m. mass at St. Joachim's. The hour concluded with Aunt Agnes and Uncle James talking with some friends they saw on Sundays. When they were done talking, Uncle James walked outside to try and catch a bus. Once he had one, he waved to Aunt Agnes and me. The bus took us to the Hellers' street. Aunt Agnes and Uncle James still were barely speaking to each other. I could sense the tension so figured it best to mind my own business.

Uncle James led the way up to the house. We could see from the dirt road that there were people everywhere in the house. People were standing around, sitting, laughing, drinking, talking, and eating. I could see this through the living room window. Uncle James knocked loud enough to be sure someone inside would hear. Surprisingly enough, Mr. Heller opened the door.

"Come on in. The party's here."

I instantly smelled the food and heard the commotion. I moved past Mr. Heller, who was standing in the doorway with a drink in his hand.

"Hey, whoa, slow down," Uncle James called after me. I could barely hear him. I was already running to see Kate and Jimmy.

"Maryanne, you're here!" Kate exclaimed. She was excited to see me, and when Jimmy caught sight of me, he was holding a baseball in his hand.

"Glad you're here, sis. Hope you're staying out of trouble." Jimmy chuckled. "Who's ready for a quick game of baseball?"

I was already pouting and said, "Jimmy, how are we going to play baseball in the house? Won't all the grown-ups be mad?"

"No, they won't know we're playing baseball. We will be careful and keep it a secret," he said, bringing his pointer finger up to his lips.

"I don't know, Jimmy. Maybe we should play another game."

Kate didn't dare say anything. She knew better than to get in the middle of Jimmy and me. So she remained quiet, listening to the two of us.

"Come on, Maryanne. Don't you want to have fun?" Interestingly enough, the last time Jimmy asked me something along those lines, both of us nearly got killed.

"Jimmy, let's do something else."

"Okay. Fine. How about hide-and-seek?"

I always liked a good game of hide-and-seek.

"You count, Maryanne, and Kate and I will hide. Go." Both Kate and Jimmy ran out of the room, off to find their hiding spots.

"Hey! Why am I counting first?" I put my head down on the bed and began counting.

"One, two, three, four, five, six ..." *I came up with the idea. Why should I have to count first?*

"Six, seven, eight ..." Well, I wasn't going to give them a lot of time; that was for sure. "Nine, ten! Ready or not, here I come!"

"Rawr!" It was Jimmy. I screamed a little as I jumped back. After a couple of seconds, he finally settled down and, looking at Mr. and Mrs. Heller's desk, asked me, "What's that?"

"I don't know. I can't read it," I said.

Jimmy took the letter and looked over it. When he was finished, I asked him to read the letter to me.

"What does it say?" I inquired.

Jimmy was staring at the letter. He looked like he had seen a ghost.

"Jimmy? What does it say?"

Jimmy, softly and quietly, read the letter to me:

December 10, 1942

Order to Report for Induction

The President of the United States

To: John Dean Heller
      Order No. 11509

Greeting:

Having submitted yourself to a local board composed
of your neighbors for the purpose of determining your
availability for training and service in the armed forces
of the United States, you are hereby notified that you
have now been selected for training and service in
the army. You will therefore report to the local board
named above at Fulton, Missouri, at 7:35 a.m. on the
26th day of February 1943.

   This local board will furnish transportation to an
induction station of the service for which you have been
selected. You will there be examined, and if accepted for
training and service, you will then be inducted into the
stated branch of the service ...

Jimmy trailed off. He put the paper down.

I had no idea what any of that meant. As I grew older, I developed a
better sense of what was happening during that time. Back in 1940, the
United States instituted the Selective Training and Service Act. This
required all men between the ages of twenty-one and forty-five to register
for the draft. Once the US entered World War II in 1941, draft terms
extended through the duration of fighting. The war had a significant
impact on the economy and workforce. This was especially true because
we were in the years after the Great Depression. As a country, the US was

still recovering from the Great Depression, and the unemployment rate was roughly 25 percent. However, with war looming and our country's involvement, the unemployment rate dropped another 10 percent.

As more men were called to fight, women were hired to take over their positions. Before the war, women were discouraged from working, but now they were being encouraged to take over what had generally been considered men's work. Of course, I know all this now. I didn't have a clue back then.

Jimmy finished the letter and finally looked up at me.

"What does that mean?" I asked.

Jimmy gave me a stern look. "It means Mr. Heller is going to fight in the war," Jimmy whispered.

For a while, we looked at each other. I had no idea what that meant but chose to keep quiet, because the look on Jimmy's face was anything but cheerful. Jimmy finally broke the silence when he said, "Maryanne, you remember back in the beginning of the month, right? When those planes from Japan killed and hurt our people on the islands?"

I vaguely remembered the event, but I did remember seeing a newspaper clipping one morning on the kitchen table. It had some planes flying in the sky, and there was a big black cloud of smoke coming off one of the ships in the water.

Then I remembered Uncle James's face when he came downstairs that morning. He looked unkempt, which wasn't out of the ordinary. I remembered him picking up the paper, opening to the first page, then closing it after only minutes, maybe even seconds of looking at it. Uncle James never said a word to me about the paper or the war. He went about his business and acted normal.

I thought this through, my only memory of the war. I didn't want to recap, so I nodded my head in agreement.

"Well, America is at war. The army must need people to fight, so they want Mr. Heller."

"What about Mrs. Heller? What is she going to do?" I asked.

"I'm not sure. The letter didn't say anything about her. Is there another letter around here?"

We began rummaging through papers on the desk.

"What does this mean, Jimmy?" I was more concerned than confused.

"I guess it means Mr. Heller is going to fight in the war."

We had completely forgotten we were playing hide-and-seek. The noise from the party downstairs traveled upstairs, and even though it was so loud, I wasn't listening to a word anyone was saying. My thoughts raced from Mr. Heller, Mrs. Heller, and ... *Kate*. She was still hiding. How were we going to explain this to Kate? We knew that with Mr. Heller away at war, Mrs. Heller would have to work. What would happen to Kate?

"Jimmy, should we go find Kate and tell—"

An anxious Jimmy cut me off. "No. I mean yes. We should find Kate, but we can't tell her about this. I'm not sure what's going on."

"What's going to happen to Kate?" I was scared now. I could feel the tears forming in my eyes.

"Don't say anything to Kate. Maybe Mr. and Mrs. Heller have a plan—you know ... something figured out already ..." Jimmy trailed off. He seemed concerned, a little scared. I couldn't remember the last time I saw Jimmy scared.

"Let's find Kate and go downstairs. It should be the new year soon."

After about ten minutes of searching, I found Kate in, surprisingly enough, the hallway laundry basket. I helped her out of the basket, pulling off the dirty clothes that covered Kate—a few socks, a pair of pants, a couple of shirts, and even some undergarments.

"Eww, Kate! I can't believe you hid in here."

Kate let out a small giggle and smiled when Jimmy approached us.

"Good one, Kate. I think I need a break from the game. Let's go downstairs."

Kate and I watched Jimmy descend the stairs, disappearing in the crowd of people in the living room. The party seemed to have grown in the short time we spent upstairs. I took a step away from the railing, suggesting that Kate and I follow Jimmy. Kate agreed, although she was looking awfully tired. I took Kate's hand, and together we walked down the steps to get lost in the massive amount of people.

In only a short hour and a half, it was the new year, 1942. I got picked up at least a few dozen times, mostly by people I didn't even know. They were all hugging me and kissing me on the cheeks, saying things like, "Happy New Year. Be good, and all that is good will come to you."

"You are so cute. May you have a healthy and safe year."

I pushed through people who continued to celebrate with their drinks, party poppers, pots, and pans, laughing, joking, and singing. I ran over to Aunt Agnes, who stopped talking the minute I got to her.

"You okay? You look tired."

I pulled myself up on Aunt Agnes's lap. I lay down on her, resting my head on the upper part of her chest by her right shoulder. Aunt Agnes turned back to the two women she was talking to and said, "I'm so sorry, but it looks like we will be heading out."

I drifted off to sleep—a sleep that felt good, refreshing, and soothing.

I awoke feeling tired. Instantly, I remembered the draft letter Jimmy found, and a cold, hard fear settled over me. It wasn't a good harbinger for the year if Kate's home situation was in jeopardy. Still, I had to get on with the day. I stretched, then got out of bed. Once I was downstairs, I saw Uncle James sitting on the sofa and Aunt Agnes across from him. Neither of them noticed me. I stood quietly listening to their conversation, and my fear grew exponentially.

"James, how can this happen? What will we do?"

"We need to get through this."

"I'm sorry I didn't talk to you. I was upset. But what about Maryanne? I'll be back at work."

"I know. There is only one other option."

At that moment, Uncle James's eyes found mine on the steps.

"What are you up to?"

Aunt Agnes looked troubled and lost. I was scared to ask what was going on, but I had to know. My name came up in conversation.

"Maryanne, why don't you come downstairs and join your uncle James and me? We need to talk to you for a little bit. Take a seat."

No. This couldn't be happening.

"Maryanne? You look pale."

"We know this is hard for you. It is hard for us too. Trust me, we don't want to be separated from each other. This is the only thing we can do right now."

"Yes. Your aunt and I are so sorry and wish we didn't have to do this right now, especially with the new year starting off."

Aunt Agnes continued, saying, "So, we will be taking you back to the shelter within the coming weeks. I know you would love nothing more than to stay here. I will be working and unfortunately will not be around as much. Uncle James and I talked this over and figured the shelter was the best place for you."

"What about Kate?" I said.

Aunt Agnes and Uncle James looked at each other hesitantly.

"Kate?"

"Is she going to the orphanage too? Jimmy and I found a letter to Mr. Heller. Is that the one you got too, Uncle James?"

"How do you know Mr. Heller got a letter?"

"Me and Jimmy found it when we were playing hide-and-seek last night at the party."

"Umm, I don't know yet what will become of Kate. I'm sure whatever the Hellers decide will be the right choice."

The Hellers had a lot of kids. Although they weren't there the weekend Jimmy and I went to visit, everyone still lived there. Would they all go to the shelter too?

"Don't worry too much."

"When will I go back to the shelter?"

"We aren't sure."

For the rest of the day and the remaining of winter break, I stayed with my aunt and uncle. I didn't want to miss anything. By the time school started back up after the break, I was in a state of grief. It could be any day now that I would have to go back to the shelter. I wasn't nearly as prepared as I thought I would be. Time passed. Soon days turned into weeks, which turned into months. Maybe Uncle James wasn't going into the service after all. I pondered torturous thoughts.

It was a warm day at the end of May. I walked home from school along the sidewalk. When I reached our house, I saw Aunt Agnes outside on the front steps. Aunt Agnes seemed distraught. I approached her cautiously.

"Aunt Agnes?"

In that split second, Aunt Agnes ran to me, pulling me close to her in one giant motion. She was hugging me like she didn't want to let go. I had a grand suspicion she knew exactly what was going on. I would be going back to the shelter. I knew it before Aunt Agnes sobbed out the words, in between tears streaming down her face.

The time had come.

Chapter 10

I felt too sad to cry, too numb, too devastated to fully understand that I really was back at the shelter with the nuns and all the other displaced girls in that part of Philly. I just stood there staring out the window of the dorm room as Aunt Agnes and Uncle James walked down the sidewalk toward the nearest bus stop. Even though I was surrounded by many girls, I felt alone. I knew Kate would be joining me soon. Uncle James had been drafted for the war, and he finally received word that he would be off to training, to be deployed over in Europe. He was scheduled to leave the first of June. He and Aunt Agnes had to get themselves ready, so they decided it best to have me get situated back in the shelter.

My concentration was broken by a girl tapping me on my shoulder.

"I remember you. You came with those people from the Services. The one lady, Elizabeth. I thought you got out of here for good. Why are you back? Something with your new family go wrong?"

The questions were overwhelming. "I guess."

"What do you mean? What brings you back here?"

"I don't know. I guess my family ... my aunt and uncle ... She got a job, and he is going to fight in the war."

"The war? That's all the way over in Europe. Japan? They were the ones who made Pearl Harbor explode. Well, that's what my sister told me. She said Japan killed a lot of people there. Is your uncle going to fight them?"

"Pearl Harbor? What's that?"

"Pearl Harbor? You mean you don't know?"

I had never heard of such a thing before. I knew that somewhere in the country, a lot of people got hurt. Some killed. That was what Aunt Agnes and Uncle James had said.

"No. I don't know."

The girl let out a sigh of bewilderment. "Pearl Harbor was where Japan hurt the Americans. They were flying planes and dropped bombs, shot at Americans working on the ships. People died. I know that our dad went to fight over there too. He was in the army for as long as I can remember. After Mom died, Dad took care of us, but he was always working and couldn't keep taking us with him. We moved all the time. Until we got here. Then Dad got deployed for something. Not this war. He wouldn't tell us. So he brought us here. That's when I remember seeing you. My sister and I had been here for a month or so. Then we saw you and your sister. Where is your sister?"

"She is supposed to be coming here soon. I don't know when."

"You don't even know when your own sister is coming? You don't know much about anything, do you?"

"Listen, I don't know 'cause no one tells me. And I haven't seen Kate since New Year's. She doesn't live with me. Okay?"

The girl took a step back.

"Okay. Sorry ... I didn't mean to make you mad. I thought you would know more about things since your uncle was going to fight. My dad always told me and my sister things. If you want to talk some more, my bed is that one over there." The girl pointed at the bed on the far end of the room.

She walked backward away from me.

"All right. Show's over. Back to your own business now."

The girls in the room stopped watching and resumed their previous activities. I was still standing near the window. I looked around, and after I decided things were back to normal, I turned to face the window. That was when I saw her. Kate. She was being carried by Mr. Heller. I watched as they approached and disappeared from view directly under the window. I could feel the slight rumble of the floorboards.

Out in the lobby, Kate started toward the steps, and that was when she saw me.

"Maryanne" was all Kate could say before I reached her and buried my face in her shoulder.

"Kate. I was waiting for you the whole time. Do you know if Jimmy is coming too?"

"I don't know. Mr. and Mrs. Heller only said you would be here. They didn't say Jimmy."

I felt my heart sink. I wanted us to be together.

"Oh. Okay. I thought ..."

I was glad I would be with my sister again. The circumstances surrounding us at this moment were not exactly the most ideal. Still I had hope that one day we would get out of here once and for all. Never to come back. I would be with my siblings—Grace too.

We stood there hugging each other until I suggested we go into the dorm room and find Kate a bed close to me. Our time at the shelter officially began.

I finished out the last month of first grade living in the shelter with my sister. So much had happened in such a short amount of time. Nevertheless, I was happy once the weather finally turned to warmer conditions.

On the last day of school, I cleaned out my desk. I noticed I had a picture of my family and pulled it out. I couldn't believe I had forgotten about it. It was buried under a bunch of papers. I admired the picture for some time and only looked away when I felt someone tap my shoulder. I saw it was my teacher, one of the nuns. I got the feeling this nun didn't like me. She was always making me go to the front of the class, even when she knew I hated attention. She made me write extra lines, and she would bang my desk with the ruler to grab my attention.

"Maryanne, you are one silly little girl. Always scared, always so quiet ... one of the most insecure kids I have ever known."

I watched her walk off toward another one of my classmates who was picking up a large pile of papers and heading toward the trash can. I couldn't hear what she was saying to the boy, but it didn't concern me. I turned back toward my desk when the final school bell for the year rang out.

Summer.

It was mid-July when I was awoken on a bright, sunny day. The sun's rays were peering through the windows. Most of the girls were still asleep, but I noticed something different. Kate was up. She was standing over me.

"Maryanne, wake up. We are leaving."

"Kate. What did you say?"

"We are leaving. Sister said for us to be downstairs before breakfast. Our new family is coming for us today."

After so many days, weeks, and months in a place, rules and habits start to rub off on you. I sat upright in a flash.

"We don't want to make Sister mad," Kate whispered before disappearing in the hallway.

I scanned the room for my belongings. Quietly, I went over to the door and made my great escape. I frantically approached Kate. Out of breath, I said, "Kate, I can't leave without my stuff! Where is it? I can't find it anywhere."

Kate stepped aside to reveal a large suitcase. I recognized it as mine and let out a deep sigh of relief.

"There you are, Maryanne. Now if you could stay put for a few more minutes. Your new guardians should be here any minute now. There will be no need for you to go back upstairs; all your things are here with your sister. So stay put," Sister Ellen said.

She was on her best behavior to not draw any unwanted suspicion about how tight a ship she ran. Sister Ellen disappeared behind the front desk, and Kate and I turned to each other.

"Do you know who we will be going with, Kate?"

Kate shook her head. "Sister Ellen didn't say. She said for us to be ready and not a minute late."

I was anxious. I was thrilled that I would be leaving this place, and hopefully for good this time around, and with Kate too. But I was nervous, as I didn't know what kind of family we would be getting. They were going to be complete strangers, and I never liked strangers.

We sat down, and in no time at all, the front door swung open. We looked around and watched as a woman entered. Sister Ellen greeted the woman, taking her hand and shaking it between her two hands.

"Welcome, welcome. This is Maryanne and Kate," Sister Ellen said. "Girls, come meet your new guardian."

I stood up, as did Kate, and together we slowly walked over to the lady. She was an older woman with white hair, and she was pretty short. She squatted down so she was at eye level with us.

"Hello, girls," she said. "I'm Mary Malon. But you can call me Nanny. Everyone does. It's so nice to meet you two!"

"Hello," I said, trying to keep my voice from shaking. "I'm Maryanne. This is my sister Kate."

"Why, hello, Kate!" Mary said, offering Kate her hand.

Kate shook Mary's hand. Mary stood up and faced the desk.

Sister Ellen said, "They will be all yours in a few moments. There is some last-minute paperwork for you to fill out. All right, now if you could fill these out for me, please."

Sister Ellen handed the forms to Mary and went back to work on some paperwork of her own. Kate and I sat back down on the bench near the desk and watched as the lady filled out the forms. When she was finished, she pushed the papers across the desk to Sister Ellen, who looked up from what she was doing with a big smile. I had never seen Sister Ellen so happy. She was usually miserable. She checked the forms.

"Well, now. Everything seems to be in order." She tapped the end of the papers on the desk to straighten them, gave us a stern look, and said, "Now, you girls behave. You hear? Do what Miss Mary tells you, and everything'll be okay."

"Yes, Sister Ellen," we said in unison.

"Good. You see that you do that."

"Thank you, Sister Ellen," Mary said. "I'll take it from here."

She reached out both hands. I took her right hand, and Kate took her left hand.

"Come on, girls," she said. "Let's go."

As we walked out of the shelter together, I realized that my life would never be the same again. Everything was changing so fast. It made my head spin. It still does, even all these years later. Although it was too soon to tell, I thought things would work out with Mary. Looking at Kate, I couldn't stop or hide my smile of happiness. Kate returned the favor to the woman by saying, "I can't wait to see my new home."

"That's the spirit, girls. Now who wants to make a quick stop at the corner store on the way home? Lots of mouths to feed. Oh, I think you two will be pleased with how many brothers and sisters you will come to grow up with. I have quite a few children in my care. It is going to be a lot at first, I'm sure, but you will get used to it. I hope you like it here."

The woman continued to talk to us. Most kids would probably think she was crazy or boring, but I loved to listen to her. She would start off talking to us, then seemed to forget she had little ones by her side. I didn't care. This woman had the personality for kids of all ages.

"So, when I got Johnny, I said, 'Listen, I am a good mother to my own kids and am sure as hell going to look after this one here.' Oh, there's the corner store."

I followed Mary into the store, with Kate's hand in mine. We hadn't been outside the shelter in many weeks. The busy store was a bit overwhelming. I noticed that the shelves were not completely stocked. I asked Mary about that.

"Oh dear," she said with a sigh. "Almost everything is rationed. The war, you know."

"Oh," I said.

After Nanny got her groceries, she led the way to the cashier. She placed her items in front of the young woman behind the counter. Nanny grabbed the plastic bags, said thank you, and went on her way, Kate and I following closely behind her.

We arrived at Nanny's house about ten minutes later. The walk wasn't too bad. But by the end, I was ready to sit down. Nanny led us in through the front door. To my surprise, a multitude of kids greeted us at the door.

There were kids sitting on the sofa, others standing in the room, some hanging over the stairs, others upstairs, and more in the other rooms.

"Settle down. We have some new friends to introduce you too. This is Maryanne and Kate. They will be living with us, so you all better be nice. You were all in this position before, and I'm sure you were scared. Be good siblings to one another. I don't want to have to send any of you back to that shelter."

By nightfall, Nanny had fed us kids—a total of twelve in the house, between her own children and the ones she had taken in. I sat in the living room, and it felt like home. I knew it had only been a few hours, but this place and Nanny and the kids made me feel welcomed, cared for, and loved.

"Maryanne, I saved a spot for you next to me."

I saw that there were a few kids in one bed. There had to be at least five of them squeezed into one bed. I didn't mind, so I made my way to my spot. I fit and immediately became warm with the covers and kids around me. I drifted off into a deep sleep, in a happy, warm, and loving new home.

Chapter 11

The rest of the summer was full of great adventures for me, Kate and our new siblings. Nanny would take us to a small farm way out on the edge of Pennsylvania. She had become very involved with the church and community, and during summers, she made it a point to visit one of the priests who spent most of his time out that way at one of the off-site rectories. We took a bus, since that was the most common form of travel. It pulled up on a dirt road, and we took off to the front of the bus, where the doors were. Nanny hollered out, "Will you kids slow down? The bus isn't going anywhere, and neither is the farm."

We were excited to run around in the open space, something we weren't used to in the city. Houses, stores, and buildings were confined to one area. Philadelphia was a large city but appeared smaller because of close living quarters.

The farm was the opposite. I jumped from the top step of the bus and landed on the dirt road. I went with the rest of my siblings, running as fast as I could to keep up. When Kate and I caught up, there was already a plan for what we would do that day. Most of the time, it consisted of games, like what we would play in front of our home. Other times, we would venture off, exploring the grounds and other parts of the farm.

"Kate? What are we doing?"

Kate turned around. She was a few steps ahead of me.

"Weren't you listening? We are going to see if there is another house out past the field."

Past the horses was a barn. I figured that was where the horses were kept, for sleeping purposes mostly but also to keep them out of any bad weather.

We became so occupied with our activities we didn't realize how long we had been outside. I looked over my shoulder to see the door open slightly.

"You kids must have had a pretty good time. You look wiped out." Nanny poked her head inside the door, then reappeared. "I think it's time to go. We have been here all morning already. It's almost two o'clock. It will take us a little bit to get back home. We should probably head home."

Nanny went back inside to say goodbye to the staff and priests in the rectory. I was the first to stand up. I took Kate by the hand and went inside to find Nanny. Slowly thereafter, kid by kid trickled into the rectory, waiting to finally leave. Nanny was finishing her conversation with one of the priests. I had never seen him before; he must have been new. The priest stuck his hand out for a shake. Nanny grabbed it and then went in for the hug. Nanny let go after a moment and then led us outside and down the dirt road. The bus was waiting for us. The driver saw us and ignited the engine. He opened the doors, and when Nanny, the last of the group, sat down, the driver put the bus in drive, eased up on the brake, and moved forward.

About a half hour passed. The sun was still high in the sky, beating down, causing the heat wave. The bus was hot. The windows were rolled down, but it was circulating hot air from the outside. I started to drift off into a light sleep. The ride was a little bumpy, but I still managed to rest. The bus grew quiet as the ride progressed. Soon everyone was asleep.

The bus was jerking everywhere. I awoke when I started to feel queasy. It was the constant motion of rocking back and forth. Fortunately, I recognized we were at least back in Philadelphia. The shops, buildings, and houses—what I saw every day—were a familiar reminder that I was almost home. The bus rolled up to the station to let the passengers off.

"All right. Now that we have everyone, let's head home."

After walking a few blocks, Nanny turned onto our street. By this time, some of us started running toward the house as the bright sun disappeared behind dark, ominous clouds. Rain started to fall. I heard some faint screams behind me. Some of the girls were getting wet. The boys started laughing and running ahead, their arms open wide. Nanny continued at the same pace. I glanced up at her to see a faint smile on the corner of her lips. That was exactly the kind of fun I had with that family. Everyone together, having a good time, even if it was in the rain. I very rarely remembered a time when I was younger, with my family, when a moment like this presented itself. By the end of the walk, we were drenched. It didn't matter to me. I was having fun. With my family.

Two years passed faster than ever. I was a few weeks away from completing the fourth grade. I had matured, even though I was at the mere age of ten. There was consistency in my life. Nanny had given me the support I needed, especially when I first started living with the other kids—my siblings, as Nanny called them.

One day, I was on my way home with some of my siblings. The six of us waited out in the schoolyard, like we always did, by the tree on the edge of the fence. Our eldest brother, David, should already have been there. Where was he? We decided to wait for him, to see if maybe he was still inside. After much time passed, the schoolyard was about deserted. Usually we were long gone before the schoolyard was empty.

"Should we go? I don't think he's coming."

We each picked up our bags to begin our walk home.

"Maybe he's sick and Nanny came to pick him up?"

"What if he's skipping school today?"

"I don't know. I hope everything is okay," I stated.

I turned the corner to walk the remainder of the street toward home when the first words were spoken in nearly twenty minutes.

"Look! What is that?"

A white van was pulling out of the driveway of Nanny's house. It pulled away before we could read the words on the van. Off in the distance, red lights started flashing. Then we heard a faint siren. Frantic now, we ran to our house. I was first, running up the front porch steps and throwing open the door with all my might.

Nanny was standing in the living room with a young man. He looked to be about thirty or so. When we entered the room, Nanny and the young man stopped talking. They both looked at us, swarming them, looking for answers. Nanny, in her calmest voice ever, told us to go upstairs or outside and run along. I gave her the wide-eyed look. I wanted to stay and find out what was going on. I had to know what happened. With everyone out of sight, we certainly were not out of earshot and could hear every word that was being said between Nanny and the young man.

"He didn't look good, Nan. It's best they took him. I know how hard it is for you, being his caregiver. But he's my son. We're as devastated as you, Mom."

Turns out, the eldest brother, David, was Nanny's grandson. Nanny had agreed to take care of him when her daughter became sick and her husband was unable to provide for him. Nanny agreed and received a small sum of money. Whenever kids were in foster care, the shelter from which they came paid the caretaker money to provide for the children. I sat and listened on the steps, trying to stay as quiet as possible so Nanny and her son-in-law would not hear. Their conversation ended with the door closing behind him. The shutting of the door was a clear indication that it was time to scatter. I moved quickly to ensure no one would see me. Once inside the bedroom, I closed the door with a soft click.

Within the next week, we were taken out of Nanny's house and placed in the shelter. Kate and I went back to the Catholic Children's Bureau.

"What happened? Do you know, Maryanne?" Kate asked the first night we were back at the shelter.

After David was taken to the hospital, within two days, everyone was out of the house. David had contracted tuberculosis.

I nodded. "He's sick. I don't know how he got sick."

"But what does he have? A stomachache? A headache? What is wrong? Why does he have to go to the hospital?"

"I don't know, Kate. That's why he went to the hospital. The doctors are going to try to figure out what's wrong. Hopefully they find out soon. I don't want to be back here again. I miss Nanny and everyone else."

"Me too, Maryanne. I want to see everyone again."

I could tell that Kate was having trouble adjusting, like me.

"You should probably get some sleep, Kate. I don't know what will happen tomorrow, but maybe Nanny will come back for us and bring us home." I turned to look at Kate, who was already lying down, eyes shut and breathing quietly. I turned to lie on my back. Tears rolled down my face while I stared at the ceiling. Nanny, our siblings, home, and neighborhood, and everything we did together flashed before my eyes. I cried myself to sleep that night. It was the first time I had done so in nearly three years.

Kate and I remained in the shelter for some time. Months passed before Kate and I started school again. I was now in the fifth grade. I'd get up, eat breakfast with the others in the shelter around the table, walk to and from school, going back at the shelter to do homework and chores until it was time to wash up for dinner and go to bed. On the weekends, there was more free time, which, in hindsight, allowed us to get into some trouble, whether intentionally or not. I remember one of the older girls, June, who did the ironing around the shelter. She took the clothes from us, ironed them, then placed each article of clothing on the respective owner's bed. I never liked June. June taunted Kate quite often, and when I tried to defuse what would have been an argument, June began taunting me as well. June would scream at me, "You are never getting out of here! Never! You will be in this shelter your whole life!"

I didn't know it at the time but, I later learned that June was living with a mental illness. She lost her temper very easily, then tended to get very aggressive. The last time I saw June, she was ironing downstairs in the laundry room. I had gone down there to drop off the rest of my clothes to be washed then pressed. June had started yelling about how I would never leave the shelter. After I gave June my clothes, I left immediately.

June was still yelling after me as I left the room, which woke Sister

Ellen from her nap. Sister was furious. She marched right into the laundry room where June was still hollering and yelled at her to "Shut up!"

June, quiet for a moment, spun around and, with her strength, coming purely from anger, threw the iron at Sister. June threw it so far and hard that it came unplugged from the wall. Hot water flew everywhere. Sister Ellen raised her hands and, in a fit of rage, charged June. It was rumored that maybe Sister killed June. Others thought that June left on her own. Then there were the rest who believed that June was thrown out of the shelter for her behavior. I remember seeing Sister come upstairs later that night. Sister was quiet, until she made eye contact with us. Sister began yelling at any of us who looked at her, with the burn mark on the side of her head and on her arm. Sister came right over to me and screamed, "You are the most insecure human being ever!"

Because of being cooped up in there for so long, the nuns agreed that when someone reached their tenth birthday, they were allowed out for one week of the shelter for Christmas and then Easter. I (and later Kate) would go to Aunt Florence's house to spend time with Jimmy and the rest of our mother's family. I savored those weeks at Christmas and Easter. I missed Jimmy terribly, and it broke my heart that Grace was growing up a stranger to us. We hardly ever saw her, and when we did over the holidays, Grace didn't act like she knew us. And she actually didn't. As more time passed, we'd grow further apart.

At Christmas, I was let out after my last day of school. Aunt Florence met me at the shelter and took me to her apartment, where Uncle Joe and Jimmy were preparing for the holiday. This year, Jimmy had his friend over, William. Jimmy officially introduced us, and I thought he was a nice boy. He was very quiet, well mannered, calm, and gentle. The two of them would go off most of the time, while I stayed close to Aunt Florence and Uncle Joe. I finished out the year with my family. Then, once school was to start back up, I returned to the shelter. I reunited with Kate, who was happy to see me and show me what she got for Christmas.

The following day, two women, Ms. Green and Ms. Brown, came to the shelter. They were both short. One had dark hair, and the other's hair was lighter in color. One wore a hat, and the other did not. They were both dressed in their best outfits to make that lasting impression with the nuns. I didn't know the difference of who was who, Ms. Brown or Ms. Green, but I would soon find out.

The woman who identified herself as Ms. Green held onto me, while Ms. Brown held Kate's hand. We left the orphanage together, out onto the busy streets of the city. We walked a few blocks to a small house on the corner. It was small in size, perfect for two older ladies who lived by themselves.

There were small sounds coming from inside the house. We continued to walk toward the house. We proceeded to go in through the backyard. A tiny sunroom was attached to the back of the house. The two women pulled me and Kate up the steps through the sunroom door. Inside the room, they let our hands go.

"This is Maryanne and Kate." She pointed respectively to each of us when she said our names. "They will be staying with us now. They come from the shelter a few blocks away from here."

Ms. Green, who addressed the kids, walked out the back door, with Ms. Brown on her heels. They went to the front of the house. There was a door that connected the sunroom to the house. It remained locked, always. We were never allowed to go in the front of the house; that was one of the rules. The kids welcomed Kate and me, filling us in on rules and what we needed to know about Ms. Green and Ms. Brown. Dinner was always apple butter bread with potato chips.

"Wait. Is that it?" I questioned.

"That's all they give us."

That was why everyone looked so skinny. That was what they were given to eat.

"How come? Is that all they have? They don't have a lot of money?"

"That's what they have. They never said anything about any other food. Never asked us what we like."

"Can we eat more if we're still hungry?"

"Depends on how much there is from the beginning. Sometimes, Ms. Green will go out to the store. Other times, there isn't enough, so we can only eat either one or two pieces each."

I pulled Kate aside to whisper to her, "Don't worry, Kate."

I wiped the tears from Kate's face.

"Okay, thanks for the help," I said to the young boy.

It was a relief that I had gotten Kate outside, as the tears still streamed down her face. Now the hard part was going to be to try to calm her down.

Kate positioned herself on the grass with her back to the house. I sat down next to her. I put my arm around her. Kate didn't move. She sat there until she softly asked me, "Will we be here forever now?"

I didn't know what to say. I didn't know for sure. Nothing was certain, ever. I could only manage to say, "It will be okay, Kate," not sure if I believed my own words. Kate didn't ask any further questions. We listened to the surrounding sounds of the city in the distance. A siren. A few dogs barking. A couple of car horns. The sun was behind a few buildings and houses. It was preparing to set. The sky was a mixture of blue, white, pink, purple, and orange. The moon was out too. It was a pretty picture, on the verge of dusk. For the remainder of the sunlight, we sat in silence, arms wrapped around each other. When one of the boys opened the back door, I turned to see his head poking from around the inside. He gestured with his hand to come inside. I tugged a little on Kate to try and get her up.

"Come on, Kate. Let's go eat. Who knows. Maybe it will be good."

The days became a blur to me. I started missing school while living with Ms. Green and Ms. Brown. I also rarely saw them. They would come to the back of the house to let us know when it was time for dinner. The only thing ever to eat was, as the one boy said, apple butter bread, potato chips, hotdogs, and beans.

Later one evening, while the house was asleep, I tiptoed to the phone that sat on the small end table. Ms. Brown and Green enforced many rules, and one was that we were not allowed to touch the phone. I picked up the receiver, hearing the dial tone. Then, even more quietly, I spun the number dial. I waited. The phone was ringing on the other end. The ringing stopped when a voice answered, "Hello?"

"Aunt Florence? It's Maryanne. Can you please come and get us out of here? I am so hungry, and I don't like it here. The ladies ... they don't let us in the house and only give us apple butter bread and chips for dinner. My stomach hurts. Please. Can you come get us?"

"Maryanne, I know it's tough. Hang in there. You're going to be okay. Anything can happen. Stay put."

"But, Aunt Florence, I don't want to live here. I don't like it here. Please come take me and Kate out of here."

Aunt Florence sighed a deep breath.

"I know, Maryanne. Please try to keep yourself together and stay strong. I know you don't want to be there. Keep going. You will get out of there soon. I'm sure of it. I have to go, but you can talk to me again tomorrow if you want."

Aunt Florence hung up the phone. The dial tone rang in my ear. I quietly placed the phone back. I stood there for a moment. I felt a pain in my stomach. I was glad to have talked to Aunt Florence but upset that I couldn't do anything to get us out of this house. I decided to sneak upstairs into the attic of the house. From there, I could see the top of Ben Franklin on city hall. With tears running down my face, I began to sing. The only words that came naturally to me were the lyrics of "God Bless America." I sang through the tears, staring through the window at the top of Ben Franklin with the moon shining brightly. Once I caught myself falling asleep, I crept downstairs back to my spot on the floor, where there was a massive pile of blankets. I positioned myself next to Kate, who was fast asleep, a few little snores coming from her.

By the end of my fourth week with the two women, not much had changed. I had been getting ready to go outside when Ms. Brown and Ms. Green came barging through the door that led from the back room to the kitchen. They started shouting things, not making any sense to me or the others. Ms. Green threw something at the door, which closed it. She pushed us out the back door. Kids were crying. A couple of men pushed their way through to the back room. Both men were in nice clothes. They were on a mission to get to Ms. Brown and Ms. Green. One man caught up to me and gently held my arm, while Ms. Brown continued to pull me.

In the commotion, he said, "Ma'am, please, let go of the child. You are making this harder than it has to be."

Ms. Brown didn't let go. She continued to hold onto me, pulling me more.

One of the men picked me up. Ms. Brown was forced to let me go. I began to cry. I had no idea what was happening. The man held me. He turned to his partner in the back room, handed me off to him, then went into the yard to gather the rest of the kids.

The noise outside settled down. The back door slammed open with the man holding Ms. Brown and Ms. Green, one with each hand.

One of the men spoke to the kids softly. "Both that man and I are partners. We work for Child Protective Services. It's time we get you kids out of here. We had some complaints from neighbors and a couple of anonymous callers. These women weren't taking proper care of you kids."

"Sorry, but what is your name?" one of the older boys asked.

The man looked at the boy with a serious face, only to say, "Don't worry about my name. Be glad you are getting out of here."

He took us back out the door into the yard. He was like the mother duck, with a bunch of little ducklings following right behind. This man was taking us to the only place, aside from Ms. Brown and Ms. Green's house, I dreaded the most. As we continued to walk up to the building, I turned back to look at Kate. With a deep exhale, I walked up the steps, still following the group of kids, following the man. He opened the door and stood behind it to allow for the children to pass him, straight into the foyer of the shelter.

Chapter 12

I was back at the shelter. This man, I now came to realize, worked for Child Protective Services, like Elizabeth. He must have been tipped off about our living situation at Ms. Brown and Ms. Green's house. The man brought up the end of the line, forcing us to go to the desk in the lobby. Sister Ellen came around from the back.

Sister nodded while she did a scan of the room, making sure to get an accurate headcount in the process.

"Thank you for your service. We have it from here."

The man bowed in respect of Sister. After a shake of his head, he turned to leave the building.

Sister escorted us upstairs.

The room was no different from when Kate and I left. The beds were still there. Girls were scattered all over the room. Although I was only gone for a month with Kate, I thought for some reason things might have changed. The girls in the room looked at the open door to see me standing there with Kate by my side.

"Maryanne? How are you?"

I wrapped my arms around my friend in return. After a quick second, my friend pulled back to show me a small scar on her arm.

"Look at this. I guess you're wondering how I got it. Well, it's a long story."

"Kate and I were with a family for a month. We got back not too long ago," I told her. "What's wrong?"

"I ... I'm leaving tomorrow."

"What? I mean ... why are you leaving?"

"I don't know. I guess I'm going with a new family."

"Did Sister say anything? Who you would be living with? Where do they live?"

She shook her head, indicating to me that she didn't have much information. We went about our business, preparing for the following day by laying out our clothes, cleaning up each of our beds so we could go to sleep, and finally saying goodnight to each other as the lights in the room went out. I drifted off to a fitful sleep filled with disturbing dreams I couldn't remember, and when I awoke with the dim light of dawn shining through the windows, I realized where I was, and I came close to tears.

"Maryanne? Wake up," Sister Ellen said.

I rolled over and looked up. The nun was standing next to the bed with a stern look on her face. "I received a call last night. You two are leaving today as well. A man by the name of Peter will be your new caregiver. He doesn't live too far, but he called last night and said he would be around today. Grab your things and bring them down."

I sat upright, set my feet on the ground, and grabbed my bag from under my bed, where I usually stashed a lot of my belongings. I filled the bag with everything. Kate was done too when I turned to tell her, "Meet you downstairs."

Back down in the lobby, we plopped on the sofa in the middle of the room.

About two hours passed. Kate sat quietly and patiently.

Boom ... boom.

It was the sound of the front door opening then closing. A man had come through the door, without any regard for his surroundings. He strolled over to Sister, who was still behind the front desk.

"Hello. I am here for ..." He trailed off as Sister pointed behind him, to the middle of the room.

"Excellent," the man said. He approached us, knelt, and looked us in the eye. "Why, hello, Maryanne. Hello, Kate."

I didn't like this. I got a bad feeling. Even though Jimmy always told me I worried too much, and most of the time I was a little too concerned, this time felt different. He didn't have a smooth or normal stride about him. He walked kind of crooked. Not like he couldn't control it, like it was his choice. That left an odd feeling in the pit my stomach. Kate didn't seem too concerned about him. Maybe I was overreacting a little bit ... again.

"Well, we best get you two home. You can join all the others. I am sure they will be happy that you are there."

Kate nodded in agreement—or obedience. I wasn't sure. However, I made no sudden movement. Something about this man gave me the feeling that he was *off*. Sister handed over forms that Peter needed to read and sign. After he was done with the paperwork, he turned it over to her, and she exchanged it for an envelope.

"Well, thank you for your time and these two lovely children. They will make a great addition with the others."

Sister Ellen was talking as the man held my hand and Kate's. I could only catch the tail end of what she was saying, for the door closed abruptly behind me. I looked up at the man, who didn't even seem bothered by the fact that the door closed as Sister was still talking.

"Jeez. Finally. I thought that would take forever. Crazy lady. Whatever. I have you two now."

He was talking to himself, and I was waiting for him to realize that Kate and I could hear everything he was saying, but he must have already known, for he continued to talk to himself the whole way.

"Oh, I'm Peter. I don't know if that fool ever told you my name. But you will be living with me. There are others of course."

I saw that he wasn't looking at Kate the entire time he was talking to us. He only looked at me or straight ahead of him. He didn't seem to pay attention to Kate. He continued to drag us along the sidewalk. We walked a great distance, maybe a few miles. When we turned one last corner, he began to slow his walk. Kate and I were nearly out of breath trying to keep up with him.

Peter brought us to a stop outside a small row house where a woman was sitting outside on the small front porch.

"You got them. Why don't you two come inside?" The woman on the porch reached out for me and Kate. Peter let us go, reluctantly. I didn't know what his problem was, but he sure had one. Kate and I followed the woman into the house. It was small, probably the smallest house I had been in so far. There was a living room on one side, the left, and the kitchen/dining area on the right. The steps leading upstairs were at the far end of the kitchen.

She left the house through the front door. Kate shrugged her shoulders at me.

"What do you think of this place, Kate?"

"I don't know. It seems okay. The lady is nice."

"What about Peter? What do you think about him?"

"Umm ... I don't know. He is ..."

"What?" I asked quickly.

"Different."

"What do you mean?"

"He isn't like Mom or Dad or Nanny or anyone else we lived with. He is different."

We followed the noise coming from down the hall. We passed two small bedrooms and a tiny bathroom. I poked my head into each room. The two bedrooms each had one bed with a dresser. One window in each room gave way to the main source of light. I walked past the bathroom, still following Kate, and stuck my head in the doorway. The bathroom was smaller than the bedrooms. The sink was next to the toilet, and there was a small tub/shower. I drew back out, still following Kate to the sound coming from the room down the hall. It was loud in the room, what sounded like multiple voices of young kids. I wondered how anyone could be living in a small house with only one bathroom.

Kate knocked on the door. The room quieted. She grabbed the door handle and pushed the door open. There in the room, I couldn't believe what I saw.

There were a total of eight girls in the room; adding me and Kate would make ten.

"Hi, I'm Kate, and this is my big sister, Maryanne. We will be living with you now."

"You two come from a shelter?"

It was my turn to talk. "Yes."

The other girls looked at one another with no facial expressions.

"Is something wrong?" I asked.

The girl who had spoken before answered, "No. We don't know why they keep bringing more of us in. There is hardly any room."

"I thought the same thing when I saw you in here," I confessed.

"Do they feed you?" Kate was curious to know, especially after our encounter at Ms. Brown and Ms. Green's house.

"They always have plenty of food for us. They let us go back for seconds and thirds too if we want. The only thing he does that you have to be careful for is when he takes you into that room. The one next to the bathroom."

"Why?" I inquired.

"It is only if you are bad. You don't listen ... Peter will take you into the room and—"

"Will you girls come downstairs for a minute?" Peter's wife interrupted. I would be sure to bring that back up again, when we had the time to, out of earshot of Peter and his wife.

"We will be right down," one of the girls said.

"I will talk to you later," she whispered as she passed by me and Kate with the others, out into the hallway. When we were in the living room, the wife spoke to us collectively.

"I would much rather say this once. Peter isn't feeling too well. Please don't bother him or do anything to make him upset. I have some errands to run, so be on your best behavior. Are we clear?"

We nodded in agreement.

"I will see you soon."

Kate and I followed the group back upstairs. We reached the room, and as soon as we did, the one girl closed the door.

"Where was I?"

"What happens when Peter gets upset? He takes you somewhere?"

"I was never back there, but one of the girls that was here before warned me when she was leaving here and I was coming in. She said to always listen to him and it won't be so bad."

"What isn't so bad?"

The girl shrugged and said, "I wish I knew, but that was what she told me, and I never saw her again. But anyway, it's nice to meet you both. The eight of us have been here together from the start. We came from different homes and shelters."

I was tired of this already. What good was it living in a home where you had to be careful? Had to make sure you didn't get Peter mad or upset? What kind of place was this? I went about the rest of the day with the other girls. Kate and I became accustomed quickly.

Peter's wife had returned by this point, and she was sitting in the dining area with him when we entered the room. I followed exactly what they were doing. I also made sure that Kate was doing the same.

I had my plate of food but stayed behind to make sure Kate was okay. Kate dropped the large spoon on the floor that had been in the pot for us to use. The spoon fell with a loud *clank*. I shuddered at the thought that Peter was in the room when it happened. I didn't have to turn around to look at him because I heard his wife say, "It was an accident, Peter. I have done that before. I will get a new one for the rest of the girls."

"I *know*, but still, she should know not to do that."

I could sense the agitation in his voice. I made eye contact with Kate, trying to hurry her along, but Kate could do nothing until Peter's wife got a new spoon. I stood close to Kate. The last few girls in line for food waited patiently and said nothing. I helped Kate finish with her food. I only stopped when I heard a voice from behind me.

"That's enough. She will do the rest. Go out in the living room, child." It was Peter. I had the sudden urge to throw the spoon and entire pot at Peter but thought otherwise when I saw Kate's face, then the few girls in line still waiting to get their dinner.

I joined the rest of the girls, who were almost done eating.

"What took you so long? Did something happen?" one of the girls asked.

I took a seat on the far side of the room.

"I'm talking to you. What happened in there? I heard something crash. Then I didn't hear anything for a couple of minutes. What did you do?"

"I ... didn't. The spoon fell out of the pot," I said.

"What do you mean? The spoon fell? How? What did Peter do? Did he say anything?"

I was reluctant to answer the insistent questions. "He told me to leave the room ... and let the rest of the girls get their dinner."

"Did he tell you to ... you know ... go in the room?"

"No. His wife was in there too. She told him it was an accident and to not worry about it. She got a new spoon."

"Wow. You got lucky. Lucky that his wife was in there. Who knows what would have happened if she wasn't. Well, you would have found out what happens in the room."

"Can we eat? I'm hungry and don't want to—" I was cut off because, at that moment, Kate and one of the other girls came into the room. While sitting there, I made a promise that I would protect Kate. Kate and the remaining girls sat down wherever they could to eat their dinner. I kept my gaze down, staring at my empty plate. I was still hungry but knew better than to go back in there while Peter and his wife were still there.

One by one, the girls finished their meal. I watched as each one got up to return their plate and utensils in the kitchen. When I turned around to leave though, Peter was looking directly at me.

"Where is the other one? Your sister?" Peter asked me.

I didn't want to talk to him.

"Where is your sister?"

I answered hesitantly, "She is still eating."

"Oh. Well you make sure she comes in here to drop off her plate when she is done. Are you *scared* of me? Why? There is nothing to be afraid of, child. I brought you both here. I *saved* you from those shelters and homes you came from. Nothing to be fearful of, child ... nothing."

"I ... will," I said to him.

"I will see you in the morning, child."

Before Kate went through the door, I softly pulled her aside. "He was asking about you. Don't say anything unless you absolutely must. I don't trust him."

Kate looked at me with her utmost attention. I knew Kate would obey what I said, but I was nervous that Peter would break her down. I let her go. Kate disappeared through the door. I listened. I couldn't hear anything in the other room.

"What took so long? What did he say to you? Kate. I'm not joking."

"Nothing, Maryanne. He told me not to do that again—you know, drop the eating utensils."

I was still skeptical.

Kate tugged at my shirt. "I'm tired."

"Fine," I reluctantly agreed.

I grabbed Kate's hand as I guided her to bed. I lay down next to her as my eyes started to droop. They felt like heavy weights, and finally I couldn't fight the weight any longer. My eyes closed, and everything went black.

A loud sound woke me. I looked around the room, but everyone was sound asleep. After a few moments, I collected my thoughts and realized I had a bad dream. I saw Kate sleeping peacefully, bundled up, and that calmed me down. I laid back down and closed my eyes, and then I heard it again—a shout coming from somewhere outside our room. My heart was pounding in my chest. I swallowed hard, then got up from my spot on the floor. I tossed my blankets aside, then tiptoed over to the door. I heard it again. It sounded fainter than the previous two, but it alarmed me. I pressed my ear against the door. Within minutes, I heard a door slam open and a soft weep coming from the other side, out in the hallway.

"See? That wasn't so bad. You deserved that. You know why."

A few sobs interrupted the voice.

"Now you get to bed. Don't come out until morning. You hear?"

The voice repeated, "I said you hear?"

I could safely assume that the voice belonged to Peter.

"Yes." It was barely audible.

"Go," Peter said.

I was fearful that I might get caught, so I tiptoed my way back to my spot on the floor. I covered myself in time as the door opened. I couldn't see who was entering the room. I was relieved that I had made it back under the covers in time. The door closed without a sound. I could make out the steps of the person by the creaks on the floor. They got into bed.

Then all was quiet. I wanted to sit up and peek at the bed. I tried to calm myself. My heart was racing. There was no way I would be calm enough to go to sleep now, even if whoever it was was sleeping themselves. Peter had taken them into that room. I knew it. What had happened in there would remain a mystery for who knew how long. Well, at least until morning, when I would have to summon up the courage to ask again what happened in that room.

It took time for me to fall asleep that night. I was hopeful about finding the answers I needed, but, alas, that was not to be. I never found out who had been in the room with Peter, and I assumed I would never find out. Kate and I began to accept that this would be our new home for the time being. I could only hope we would leave sooner rather than later. I looked forward to leaving the house whenever I could, mostly the days when I had school. In fifth grade, I developed good relationships with my teachers. I did my best to stay out of trouble.

The teachers would look at me with a smile, but some of them didn't truly buy my story. A couple of them wanted to look into what was going on in my life outside school. Most of them knew I was living in a foster home. On a few instances, a handful of the teachers investigated my background. They asked more questions. Then everything changed one day early in the morning just as we were sitting down for breakfast. I was seated at the table next to Kate when Aunt Florence burst through the front door.

Peter stood up from table, his face taut with rage. "Who the hell are you?" he asked. "And what are you doing in my house?"

Aunt Florence ignored him. "Maryanne. Kate. You—"

"Aunt Florence!" I exclaimed. "What are you—"

"No time for questions. You two are coming with me."

Aunt Florence pulled us up from the table.

"Hey, you can't do that!" Peter said, coming around from behind the table.

Aunt Florence turned on him. "You watch your step, buster. You're in real hot water. Only you don't know it yet."

I noticed that Peter went a bit pale.

"What about—"

I was cut off again by Aunt Florence. "No time for talking or questions."

She pulled us out the front door before Peter could interfere.

"But what about our stuff?" Kate asked.

"Never mind that," Aunt Florence said.

Chapter 13

"You two will stay with me tonight. Then tomorrow, or whenever we can, we will get you to ..." Aunt Florence trailed off.

"What? You will get us to what?"

Aunt Florence looked as if she was contemplating whether she should say anything or not. Finally, she said, "We will make sure this doesn't happen again. I can't believe the shelter let *him* take you both in. He is an animal."

"Why? What did he do, Aunt Florence?" I persisted.

Aunt Florence brushed off my question. "We will have time to talk later."

Soon we were at my aunt's apartment complex. Strangely, it looked smaller than I remembered it. Aunt Florence brought us inside. She immediately began to prepare a sleeping area for me and Kate, even though it was still morning. She had pillows, blankets, and cushions from the sofas. She finished setting up and saw us looking at her with confused stares.

"Like I said, you will be here for the night. Tomorrow, I think you will be going back to the shelter. Maybe. We will have to see how everything plays out."

"We are going back? Why?"

"Uncle Joe and I can't..." Aunt Florence put her head down. She sobbed softly. "I'm sorry ..." Aunt Florence trailed off again. She turned around to face the hallway, leading to the back bedrooms. She sobbed a little more as she walked away, her head down, her hands covering part of her face. She stopped, turned around, and fought back the tears. She said, "You girls stay inside the apartment, okay? There are a lot of bad people out there. I want you to be safe."

"We will, Aunt Florence," I said.

After she went into her bedroom, I turned to Kate and asked, "You didn't see Jimmy around, did you?"

Kate shook her head no. I took another quick glance around the room.

"I haven't seen Uncle Joe either. Maybe he is with Jimmy somewhere. I don't know what, but there's something going on," I said.

We passed a long, boring afternoon, ate dinner, and went to sleep in the living room. We were half-asleep when there was a large bang in the hallway. I gasped. I didn't know what it was or if it was a person. I thought it was Aunt Florence. I heard the door shut quietly. The footsteps were moving around the room. The curiosity was building up to its breaking point. It was a boy figure that I could make out. I wasn't 100 percent sure, but I thought the odds were leaning more that way. *Jimmy.* I was very much tempted to get up and run over to him, but I fought the temptation.

I watched Jimmy, hoping he would notice me. Unfortunately, he didn't. He walked around the room to the kitchen area, got a drink of water, then made a beeline right for one of the rooms down the hallway. He went inside and shut the door. I sat up in my makeshift bed. Kate slept soundly beside me. I decided to get to the bottom of this. I crept to Jimmy's bedroom and quietly opened the door. It was totally dark in the room. I couldn't see him, but I could tell there was someone asleep in the bed, and I thought it was a little strange that he'd be asleep so quickly after entering the bedroom.

"Jimmy? Jimmy? You awake?"

Nothing.

The figure stirred. It made me jump with a gasp.

"Hello? Who's there?"

I regained my composure. "Jimmy? Is that you? What's going on?"

Jimmy answered very softly, "It's me. What are you doing here, Maryanne? Have you seen Aunt Florence? Uncle Joe?"

"Aunt Florence came and got us from the foster home. She says the man is a bad person."

"Yeah," Jimmy said. "She called the cops on him. Says he's in big trouble for child abuse."

I'd known something was off about him, and now I was vindicated. "I don't know what's going to happen with us now," I said, feeling sad. "I don't think Aunt Florence knows either. What were you doing out so late?"

"I was with some friends."

"Friends?"

"We were hanging out ... lost track of time. Now I'm beat. Go get some sleep. We can talk in the morning."

I said okay and crept down the hallway to the living room. I could hear bits of conversation coming from my aunt's bedroom. I stopped by the door and strained to hear what was being said.

"Yes, I tried ... but can't ... it is better that they go back ... believe me I would love to have them here ... not enough room."

"But ... make it work ... we need to, Florence."

Fearing that I'd be discovered somehow, I kept going. I knew my aunt and uncle were talking about what to do about me and Kate, and it made me feel sad. I was also a little angry, even resentful, toward Jimmy. Why did he have a nice place to live, and we were shunted from one horrible place to another? It just didn't seem fair. It was pretty dark in the living room, with only the ambient light from the street illuminating the space. Kate was still sound asleep on the other side of the living room. I followed the path directly to my spot, then covered myself in blankets and rolled over onto my side.

I couldn't believe where we ended up.

"No, Aunt Florence." I would rather have been anywhere else than right there. Even Kate was putting up a fight. She was standing firmly in her spot, not letting Aunt Florence bring her indoors. We stood outside the tall double doors. I looked around. I noted the street sign on the corner said Twenty-Ninth and Allegany Avenue. Aunt Florence, with her hands on her hips, gave me and Kate a narrow stare. I glared back, standing my ground. Kate was glaring at Aunt Florence, who didn't seem to notice. Aunt Florence was too busy keeping her eyes and thoughts on me. With one quick, swift motion, Aunt Florence grabbed me and Kate, each with one of her hands. She held on tightly, not letting go as we both struggled to be released from her grip. Once inside, I knew there was no way out. Aunt Florence had won the battle. Kate and I were still under Aunt Florence's grip when she made her way up to the desk.

"Seeing you ... again," the nun behind the counter remarked. Aunt Florence nodded in reply. I looked up at her and noted the familiar expression on Aunt Florence's face. I knew she was fighting back tears.

Aunt Florence gave the nun a stern look before turning to us. Kate began to weep. I was able to hold it together. I knew if Aunt Florence saw us both crying, she wouldn't be able to keep back her tears any longer. Aunt Florence gave us a combined giant hug. I didn't want to let go. I could feel the hug ending. Aunt Florence pulled away and stepped back.

"I have to go, girls. Do as you are told. I love you both."

I was so caught up in the moment with Kate and Aunt Florence that I didn't realize I had never seen the nun behind the counter before. I looked around the room. Everything seemed different. After a few moments of scanning the room, I concluded that this was an entirely different shelter than before. Kate must have noted the same, because I felt her lift her head up off my shoulder and look around. Kate was quiet, which meant she was no longer weeping.

"Are you okay? Do you want to go see your room?"

Startled by the nun's voice, I spun around to face her.

"Are you okay?" the nun repeated.

"Yes."

The nun moved out from behind the counter. Taking us by our hands, the nun guided us down a long hallway. When we finally reached the end of the hall, the nun led us into our new bedroom. Kids ran throughout the hall, played catch, threw things, hung out, and laughed. The nun pushed open the last door down the hall for me and Kate. I set foot inside the doorway first, followed directly by Kate. There were a few girls in the room, who stopped what they were doing to look at their new guests. The nun smiled and gestured for me and Kate to proceed into the room. We seemed to be caught in a never-ending cycle of upheaval, misery, and despair.

I started high school, and at one point, Kate moved to another orphanage. It wasn't until I completed my sophomore year of high school at St. Margret's Vocational School that Kate was brought back to the home. I started my junior year, while Kate commenced her freshman year. We remained very close. We were allowed out of the home when the holidays came around, a week for Christmas and week for Easter. I loved those couple of weeks away. I loved them so much my entire year revolved around those weeks. It was during that time that I would go down to the village on Frankford Avenue. We were only allocated a certain amount of time, a few hours. We would arrive sometime in the late morning and usually stay until close to suppertime. Once I was in high school, I reaped the benefits. We were given more freedom. We could go to the city without the nuns or any adults. However, we were never allowed to go alone. If we were caught alone in the city, and word got back to the nuns, we were in for a rude awakening. It was during those times that I started to notice boys. One week during the holidays, a group of girls from the home and I ran into some boys from North Catholic High School. A few of the girls started going with some of the boys, meeting every day. I recognized one boy. He hung out with my brother, Jimmy. Well, at least I knew he used to. I wasn't entirely sure he still did; nevertheless, I rarely even interacted with him. He was always with a group of his friends. I usually kept to myself around boys. I tended to be shy around them. I didn't know why though. I thought they were nice, but I was not into them in any other way.

"One of those North boys likes you," a girl in my group whispered to me. "He is one of the most popular boys at North. He plays basketball and is probably going to go to college."

I was stunned. "Which one?"

"Dan McCarthy," my friend said. "And oh, is he cute or what?"

"Really?" I felt my heart rate increase.

A couple of days later, we were hanging out, and my friend spotted Dan with a bunch of his friends.

"Look," she said, nudging my right arm. "It's him! It's Dan!"

I glanced toward the group of boys, noted my brother was with them, and focused on Dan. He was gorgeously handsome.

"He's coming over here," my friend said.

And a minute later, Dan stood before me. He smiled broadly and offered his right hand. "Hi, I'm Dan McCarthy. Friend of your brother's. He's told me a lot about you, Maryanne."

"I hope all good," I said with a nervous laugh.

"Oh yeah. All good for sure."

We walked off to the side to talk a little more. I was nervous, but my anxiety decreased as we talked. He asked me out on a date as we walked towards the soda fountain. I said I could go but that my time was limited because of the shelter's rules. He said he knew all about the shelter and thought it was terrible we had to live there. We made arrangements to get together. I rejoined my group, and he rejoined his. I was really excited. I'd been asked out on my first date, and that somehow seemed to be a big deal.

Jimmy sauntered over to our group. "Hey, sis! Fancy meeting you here. Long time no see!"

"Jimmy! I'm so happy to see you!" I said, giving him a hug.

"I see that the nuns let you out today."

"Yeah, them and their stupid rules. I can't wait to get out of that hellhole," I said, kicking at the sidewalk with the tip of my right foot.

"I don't blame you," he said. He sighed and shook his head. "I always felt bad that I got to live with Aunt Florence and Uncle Joe, and you and Kate got the shaft."

I was silent for a long moment. I'd not yet come to grips with the anger I felt about the way things worked out. "I know it wasn't your fault," I said quietly.

"I know you know. But I wanted to say so anyway."

Changing the subject, he laughed and said, "Hey, so Dan says he asked you out on a date, and you said yes. Good going, sis!"

If I could have seen my face in the dim light of the street, I know I'd have been blushing beet red. "I only said yes because my friends said he was nice."

"They're right. Dan's a good guy."

"Have you heard from Dad?" I asked. I wasn't sure why I asked that. I didn't hate him, but I didn't love him either.

"Nah," Jimmy said. "Don't know if he's dead or alive, and I don't give a damn either way. Last I heard, he was living on the streets and panhandling for his booze."

The harshness of his words surprised me. I sighed and said softly, "I'm sorry to hear that."

One of Jimmy's friends came up to him and said, "Jimmy, we have to go."

"Be right there."

"Be safe and see you on Christmas." Jimmy ran across the street to meet up with his friends. I watched him go around the corner until he disappeared from view.

The time in between my encounter with Jimmy and Christmas dragged. I figured it was because I was looking forward to it. When Christmas finally arrived, I couldn't have been more thrilled.

Kate and I visited with Jimmy, Aunt Florence, and Uncle Joe for my favorite holiday. I always looked forward to the holidays, and when they were over, I immediately looked forward to Easter.

I returned to school for the second half of my junior year in 1952. I was seventeen, and Kate was in the second half of her freshman year. The nuns wasted no time assigning us chores around the shelter. We completed our chores in between homework and other duties the Sisters bestowed upon us.

Another girl and I were assigned to work together on chores for the day. We got to talking, and I found out that she had spent time with the same man Kate and I had lived with.

"He was gross," the girl said. "He never listened to anyone. He always did what he wanted to ..." She trailed off. I had a hunch I knew what she was talking about but kept quiet.

"When did you get here? The shelter?" I asked.

"I got here a little after that junkie was arrested. I was one of the last kids to leave that place."

"He was arrested? When? How did it happen? Where is he? Which jail?"

"I don't have the answers. I know he was arrested, and after that, the kids, along with me, were taken out and placed in here."

Another girl walked by us as we were completing our chores, and I caught her glare out of the corner of my eye. I didn't care at that point.

"I know my aunt called the cops on him for child abuse. Or at least that's what my brother said."

"More like sex abuse," she said.

I wasn't surprised. I was grateful that Aunt Florence got us out when she did.

"That was probably when he was taken in for questioning. He wasn't arrested then. It wasn't until a year later that he was finally arrested."

"A year? Why so long?" I stopped what I was doing. My mouth was nearly on the floor.

"Not sure. I think it was because there wasn't enough evidence to slam the guy. He was such a creep. I am glad they got him," my friend said.

"That is something. I'm glad he's locked up too. He didn't like my sister very much." I resumed sweeping the floor and was about ready to grab the dustpan.

"We better get a move on. If the nuns see us slacking off, you and I both know what happens."

Spring, like the saying goes, came in like a lion. Kate and I endured the dreaded walks from school back to the shelter in the pouring rain, sometimes even thunderstorms. It was the beginning of April, and I was preoccupied with the upcoming dance. Dan and I had gone on a couple of dates over the holiday break. We hit it off. When he asked me to go to the spring dance, I said yes without hesitation.

Now that April had arrived, I had my dress ready; it was hanging up in the closet, untouched since I got it. I wanted it to be in the best condition possible. When the day finally came, I had the girls at the shelter help me get ready.

"This is such a pretty dress, Maryanne. Where on earth did you get it?"

"I got it in the village, over the holiday break."

"That must have cost a fortune. Where did you get the money for it?"

I was reluctant to answer. Jimmy had given me some extra money, saying he wanted his sister to be the best-looking girl at the dance. He told me not to worry about paying him back. He had a job now and could afford these things, he told me.

I was extremely lucky and thankful for Jimmy's generous gift.

"I ... well ..."

"Oh!" a bunch of the girls in the room said in reaction to seeing me. I was ready for the dance now—dress, hair, and makeup done. The girls in the room were so impressed. I was finally ready but a little nervous.

"Well, don't you look nice, Maryanne. There is a boy downstairs waiting for you," one of the nuns said.

With a quick glance behind me, I saw the girls in the room staring at me with smiles. Even Kate was grinning. I felt my face turn red. I forced myself to smile back. I followed the nun down the hall, where I saw him. His back was to me as he looked around the room. I stood there for a moment until the nun cleared her throat rather obnoxiously, and that was when he turned to see me. He was very handsome, in gray dress pants with a matching gray jacket and white collared shirt, unbuttoned at the top around his neck. He stood staring at me as I slowly walked toward him. When I finally reached him, he was standing there waiting for me, with his arm stretched out. I took his arm, locking mine around it. He escorted me to the door, then out onto the sidewalk and into the car.

Chapter 14

My senior year of high school arrived on schedule. What was different was that I was now going to a new school. *Perfect timing,* I thought. I would much rather have stayed in my old school, so I could at least see my sister and friends. Things always had a way of turning upside down on me, but I didn't let it affect me. I waited on my first day out on the steps of the home. I was informed that someone would be giving me a ride to my new school, which I still hadn't learned the name of yet. After what felt like five minutes, a tiny black car pulled up to the sidewalk. I figured this was my ride when the driver stuck his head out the door, calling to me.

"Maryanne? It looks like I am your driver to take you to your school …" He trailed off as he looked down at a piece of parchment he had scribbled on. "St. Hubert's. Yes, that is the one."

Even though the driver was speaking loudly, I could only make out so many words because of the traffic noise. When I closed the door, the driver turned to look back at me and said, "You can sit up front if you like. I don't bite."

I smiled and looked forward, out the front windshield. The driver took that as his cue to turn back around and focus on the task at hand, driving me to school.

About ten minutes into the ride, the driver broke the silence, saying,

"I'm Ernie, by the way. I guess I should have told you that before you got in the car. Or at least before we started driving."

I looked at him through the rearview mirror. Our eyes locked, and I, being the shy and quiet girl, gave Ernie another smile and looked out the window next to me. Time passed. We wove through traffic until we arrived in front of the school.

"Well, it looks like we have arrived," Ernie said.

He stopped the car and waited for me to get out.

"Thanks, Ernie. See you at three o'clock." I took a deep breath, grabbed my bag, and walked up to St. Hubert's High School for Girls. This was it, my senior year of high school. I couldn't seem to get that thought out of my head. I wondered frequently what would happen to me once I graduated. I shook my head to rid myself of worry and doubt. My main focus was to find my classroom. I pulled the schedule out of my bag to try to figure out what class I had first: English Literature.

The day passed quickly. I thought I might like this school. I considered that as I exited the building at the end of the day and went to the designated pickup area to wait for Ernie.

As much as I tried to get the thought out of my head, my mind kept drifting to worries of what would happen next year. I needed to talk to Kate, maybe see her when I got back to the shelter. Squinting in the sunlight, I saw the tiny black car with Ernie in the front. He gave a friendly wave to me.

"Hey there. How was your first day?" Ernie asked as soon as I sat down, closing the door.

I looked down at my shirt and said, "It was good. Nothing special."

"Oh. Come on. I know senior year is better than good. You are about done. Getting ready for the real world now."

I gave a nervous chuckle in response to Ernie's comments. That was exactly what I was trying to avoid.

"Twenty-Ninth and Allegany. Here we are. See you tomorrow?"

"Thanks, Ernie, and yes. Tomorrow, same time. See you in the morning."

When I was out of the car, I watched him drive away. Only this time, I felt worse than I had that morning. My first day was done. In the books. Only 179 more days—179 days to figure out my life.

Inside the shelter, I plopped down across my folded laundry I had placed on the bed.

"Are you okay?" One of the many girls I shared a room with was lying on her bed, which was next to mine.

"I'm fine."

"Are you sure? You look a little sick."

"No."

"Was your first day okay? Did something go wrong?"

"Everything at school was surprisingly fine. I mean, I miss St. Margaret's, but it was fine. That's not what I'm worried about."

"What is it then?"

"What's going to happen after I graduate? Will I still be stuck here? And even if I do get out, where will I go? How will I survive?"

"Maryanne, you can't worry about all those things, at least not yet, because you still have a whole year ahead of you. Anything can happen in the blink of an eye. It will be okay. Trust me. It all takes time. You can't expect to have all the answers overnight."

"How can you be so sure? How?"

"Trust me."

I was finishing my first semester at Hubert's. Looking at my report card, I got three Bs and two As. Not bad for a new school. This was good news, but I was ready to be on break. I was simply excited for my last day of school for the year. When the bell rang, dismissing us girls, I bid goodbye to my new friends and waited for Ernie to pick me up. I was more talkative to Ernie now. We talked about our plans for the holidays on the ride to the shelter. Ernie mentioned his family, and I mentioned mine. He pulled up to the home, and instead of sitting in the car, waiting for me to exit the vehicle, he got out and met me on the other side. I looked at him, rather confused, but smiled.

"Happy holidays. Enjoy," he said, pulling me in for a hug. "See you after the new year." He ran back around to the driver's side. He got in, gave his usual friendly wave, and pulled out into traffic. I lost sight of him within seconds. His car blended in with the other cars.

Christmas Eve arrived, much to the excitement of me, Kate, and the girls in the shelter. I awoke around eight o'clock, and oddly enough, I was one of the first girls up in the room. The sooner I finished my chores, the sooner my break would start. By the time the rest of the girls were awake, including Kate, I was waiting by the front door.

"Hey, Kate. You ready? I finished your chores so we could get out of here. Don't tell anyone. I don't want word to get back to the nuns."

Kate came back a few moments later with a packed bag.

"Let's go," I said, with Kate trailing right behind me.

When the bus pulled up to the stop, Kate and I gathered our things and disembarked onto the curb. The bus drove away, and off in the distance, I could see Aunt Florence and Uncle Joe's house.

Both Kate and I were welcomed with hugs and kisses. Aunt Florence swarmed us the second we walked through the door.

"It is so great to see you both," Aunt Florence said, still hugging me. Uncle Joe was standing in the doorway, leaning on one hand, his leg crossed over the other.

"Good to see you two," Uncle Joe said with a smile. He had aged, I could tell, since the last time I saw him. He had white hairs lining his ears, his face looked worn and wrinkled, and he was wearing his glasses. Aunt Florence finally released me, and when I took a step back, I noted her aging features too—some white hair, wrinkles, and a worn face. Nonetheless, Aunt Florence had a warm smile that brightened up the room.

"Why don't you stay awhile? I'll take your bags."

Aunt Florence led the way into the living room, where I saw the backs of two boys' heads. One turned around when he heard us enter. He had dark hair, and that was all I needed to know to tell who he was right away. The boy, well, technically young man, nudged the other boy on the arm and said, "Jimmy, your family is here."

Jimmy rounded the sofa and embraced me and Kate at once.

"Missed you two," Jimmy said before letting us go. "You guys know who this is. It's my friend William."

I locked eyes with him. I felt myself blush, but he didn't notice because he had looked down at his feet.

Jimmy stated, "Bill, why don't you come around?"

Bill made his way around the sofa, as Jimmy had, and shook hands with me and then Kate.

"It's good to see you again."

After Bill let go of our hands, he started back around to the other side of the sofa, appearing to keep a safe distance for some reason.

"I'm going to start with dinner. Everyone, make yourself at home," Aunt Florence said before disappearing into the kitchen.

We sat and talked for a couple of hours until Aunt Florence called everyone in for dinner and William left for his own family dinner.

"You are more than welcome to stay, Bill. We have plenty of food," Aunt Florence said.

"Thank you, Mrs. Lyter, but my family is expecting me. I best go home. Thank you again for the offer and invite. Maybe next time."

I noticed how soft-spoken, polite, and gentle Bill was while speaking to Aunt Florence. He had a lot of respect for his elders. I admired that quality very much. Dan, my first beau, was a great guy, but I knew it wouldn't ever be serious between us.

When Aunt Florence rejoined the table, I saw her fold something and tuck it in her pocket. *Peculiar*, I thought. We gathered around, held hands, and said grace. My stomach was rumbling throughout the entire prayer. I was ready to eat.

After dinner came dessert—apple pie and Aunt Florence's homemade cookies. The food was delicious. I couldn't remember the last time I'd eaten a meal so good. Kate and Jimmy were enjoying the food too.

As the night was winding down, Aunt Florence stopped me in the hallway, on the way back to the bedroom.

"Maryanne," Aunt Florence whispered. "I have something for you." She reached into her pocket to pull out a small piece of paper.

I recognized the paper as the piece Aunt Florence had tucked in her pocket.

"It's from Jimmy's friend William ... or Bill," she said with a roll of her head. "He wanted me to ask if you could write to him. He will be leaving for Korea in a few days, after the new year. With the war going on over there, why not start 1953 off by talking to him, right? He was here on a small break. They let the boys come home for the holidays. He had mentioned you before, the last time he was here. He had seen your picture—your school picture I have out on the table.

"Here. This is the address you can reach him at, if you write to him." Aunt Florence handed me the paper, which was folded over.

"Thanks, Aunt Florence." I could feel my face getting hot. It was probably as red as a tomato. It also didn't help that Aunt Florence was staring at me. "I think I am going to write him."

"You should. He is a very nice young man and friends with your brother—even better." Aunt Florence gave me a smile, turned around, and walked back to her bedroom. I was still standing in the hallway, holding the piece of paper. I looked up and down the hallway in case anyone else might be lurking nearby and then went into the bathroom, quietly closing the door behind me. Inside the bathroom, I flicked the light on and opened the folded paper. I looked at Bill's writing. It made me smile. It was very neat—too neat for a young man. What he wrote made my smile spread.

Maryanne,

I will be stationed in Korea until next year, 1954. After I am discharged, I hope to see you, if you would like. Please write soon.

William

At the bottom of the brief note, I saw the address to contact William. I would write him. And as often as I could. William was a nice young man, I knew. Oddly enough, I had this feeling he would be more than a friend. I was going to marry him. I knew it.

In the coming weeks, winter was in full blast, and it lasted all through January, February, and into March. An arctic air had settled over the Philadelphia region, making it bitter and impossible to go outside. Snow had fallen as well, a decent amount to cause delays in the roads, school, and the workplaces. Back at home, I began to write Bill in Korea. As soon as he was deployed, I wrote him a letter. I didn't talk much about William to anyone in the home. I kept it to myself. I thought, *No one needs to know my business.* The interaction between the two of us lasted for months, even after I graduated from high school.

My graduating class was small; nonetheless, I was done and had my diploma. I had a job lined up, which I would be starting the Monday of the following week. I felt like I was in a better place, getting my life in order. The only thing that seemed to throw a wrench into my day-to-day life was the fact I was dating a young man by the name of Ben Dubs. I was still talking to William but didn't know what our official label was, since we were only writing letters to each other. I didn't know for sure if, when he came back, he would ask me out. I did like Dubs. He was charming, polite, and intelligent. He had big plans for his future, he kept telling me.

"When the time is right, I hope to start my own business. Right here in Philadelphia. Take after my grandparents, who ran their own business in auto mechanics for thirty-nine years."

Dubs came to my graduation and sat with Aunt Florence, Uncle Joe, Aunt Agnes, and Uncle James. Kate and Jimmy attended as well. When I was called up to get my diploma, I could hear Jimmy cheer.

I sat back down in my seat, holding my diploma, smiling from ear to ear. I had done it. I was done with school. No more homework, tests, or projects; it was done for good.

My family was in the stands. I spotted them and gave a wave from under my gown. They waved back with huge smiles—not as big as mine, but I knew they were happy. I was allowed out of the shelter that night, so my family treated me to dinner.

"Congrats, Maryanne. Well done. Now you are entering the real world."

"Thank you. I'm glad I can share this dinner with you all," I said.

My aunts were getting choked up. I knew someone was bound to. I had a hunch it would be my aunts. Dubs had given me a present, a necklace, and he had told me many times that he had saved up his money so he could give me a nice gift. The necklace was beautiful. I wore it for the rest of the dinner and evening.

When I returned to the shelter that evening, I wasn't sure of the exact date I would be leaving the home for good, but it would be soon. I would be starting my job Monday, and once I started making money, I might be able to afford living on my own. I was eighteen, going on nineteen in a few months. It was time to move on from my life at the shelter. Monday couldn't come soon enough.

Printed in the United States
By Bookmasters